2012AD

Severed Press

A Severed Press Book
Published by arrangement with the authors
This anthology © 2010 by Severed Press
www.severedpress.com

ISBN: 978-0-9806065-7-7

Contents

Frame of Reference

By Lyn Cannaday

"I really think this will work. I've thought it through from every angle, and it all fits," William told his wife as he drove through the desert. The ragged tufts of dry grass and the pale green cacti that lined the two lane highway were nothing more than colors streaked against the gray because he was driving much faster than his wife would have approved of.

"I gave your organ to the church. I hope you don't mind, but I thought they should get some use out of it." He didn't cry. He hadn't cried when the priest came to supervise the workers, speaking about loss and forgiveness and love as if he knew what any of those words meant. That priest with his celibacy and his white collar and his soft words didn't understand anything about losing part of your soul.

He shook his head, unwilling to sully his remaining time with Renata by having those thoughts. "I miss hearing you play in the evening. Remember

how Old Whitman would yell about the noise?"
William chuckled, but it was a humorless sound. "He
died. Heart attack. I guess when I get you back, we'll
get him back too, huh?"

Glancing over, William wasn't surprised to see
Renata sitting beside him, her smile as wide as ever.
He carefully didn't look down to see her stomach
ripped open, the wound a grotesque imitation of her
smile.

"Soon, love. I promise it will be soon."

The chain link fence appeared—the razor wire
loops along the top glittered in the rising sun. Those
metal links caught the sun and threw it in all
directions. A guard stepped out of his little guard house
with the bullet-proof glass and concrete barricades. He
held his weapon up defensively even though he must
recognize William's car. When William stopped and
rolled down the window, the morning air was still
sharp with winter chill.

"Dr. Barros," the guard said without emotion.
William liked the guards because they were honest
about their lack of emotion. Where others feigned
feelings, they had clipboards and guns and procedures.
They were as honest as nuclear particles going about
their daily tasks.

"Good morning," William offered, waiting as a
second guard rolled out a mirror that slid along the
ground on little wheels. The second guard circled the
car, searching under it for explosives. He'd missed this
routine. Trapped in rooms of weeping people and
platitudes, he'd longed for this cold efficiency.

"Badge?" the first guard asked. William
surrendered it and waited as the guard ran the
magnetic strip through a handheld reader to make sure

2

the computer still allowed him onto the site. The computer chirped at the guard, and the guard obediently gave the badge back—just like the good little piece of mindless wood he really was.

"Thank you, sir," he said. That was their ritual for ending this encounter.

"Have a good day," William finished the liturgy. He was more careful about his speed now. The first buildings were three miles inside the fence, but every action and every deviation from the rules were monitored inside the base. Renata still rode beside him, her stomach bleeding and the child inside her always dying, but he couldn't look at her; he couldn't risk having the others suspect anything. Not now. It was December 21st and he only had to reach his goal before all this was over.

As always, the elevator reminded William of a coffin ride deep into the center of the earth. Everything in the elevator was square—the square inset light, the square buttons, the square door. William always felt like he didn't fit in the elevator—he had too many curves to stand neatly in its mathematical perfection. His hair was receding in arcs, his stomach just starting to curve out so that he looked like a younger version of his father. Cyclical. All life was cyclical, and yet so many refused to see the truth that William had discovered. This truth, as much as his asymmetrical curves, made him feel like he didn't fit the geometrical perfection of this place.

The door opened with a chirp. "Dr. Barros." In the hall, Paul Marconi waited with an unctuous smile. That unfamiliar emotion on the old man's face trapped William in the elevator. He didn't want to get any closer to a fake smile offered up on an altar of politeness. But Dr. Marconi ignored William's distress. "I'm glad to have you back. I can't tell you how sorry we all were about your wife. She was a beautiful woman."

William hesitated so long that that the doors began to close again, and he had to put out a hand to interrupt their ritual. Interrupting their mathematically determined ritual made him feel a little guilty, so he stepped off to allow the elevator to return to its task. "Thank you," he said woodenly.

"I'm just glad to see you back. You have a lot of support here." Dr. Marconi walked beside William as they travelled the long hall to the main control rooms. Little gold and red balls were a mute testimony to the season, and someone had stuck up a cardboard cutout of a menorah. William didn't match the perfect curves and pi ratios of those gaudy balls any more than he matched the precise and gray lines of the halls.

"If you need anything, more time off perhaps, a number of people have expressed a willingness to donate some of their personal days."

William glanced over and wondered what Dr. Marconi was thinking. He was an old man, his face drawn down by gravity and his hair thinning to a crown of white wisps. In the past, Marconi had ignored William, dismissed him as the young upstart with a degree and no real talent. Marconi was the generation who had built this facility. He had written computer programs with perfect numbers that would protect the country, and he considered the ones who came now as nothing more than glorified window washers. In the past, he'd never bothered to hide that opinion.

"Thank you," William answered when Marconi looked over at him with a frown. "I think I'd rather be working."

"After that trial, I can understand why." Marconi placed a warm hand on William's arm, and William shivered at the human contact. His mind conjured the warmth of Renata's blood-stained hand as she grabbed his arm. She hadn't been strong enough to scream, so she'd mouthed words of prayer. Her other hand was splayed out over her swollen belly. He'd shivered then, too. He'd shook so hard that it took three tries to dial 911.

William blinked away the memory. "I just want to get back to work." He didn't want the work as much as he needed it. If the universe failed today the way it had failed when Renata died, he would never see her again. It was his job to make sure the numbers balanced.

"Your numbers always balance, William." Marconi patted him on the arm before turning back toward the elevator and heading down the hall. His footsteps ticked off the seconds as William stood outside his lab with his heart racing with panic. He replayed the conversation in his mind. What had he said to Marconi? Had he revealed himself? Did Marconi know? Maybe Marconi with his numbers had already seen the truth... maybe he recognized William's need to take his place in the universe's perfect ritual of rebirth.

With his own imperfect knowledge, he had no way to know, so he could only follow the plan. When he slid his badge into the slot, the door slid open for him. Inside, long tables stood in perfectly straight lines, each with a dozen monitors set into the surface.

"William."

He turned to see Beth Daniels walking toward him. "William, I'm so very sorry. Did you get the flowers? I know they don't help anything, but I wanted you to know that all of us were thinking about you."

William looked around. George was standing near his workstation, his face twisted into an unfamiliar frown. Aizel had swung her chair around to face them, and Jimmy was standing in the middle of the room after taking one step toward William and then stopping. William's own workstation was at the back of the room, near the door where he could face the others. Someone had placed a little tree made out of silver-wrapped chocolates on the edge.

The faces were all so familiar, but he didn't know them anymore. They'd known Renata's husband, and it had been Renata's husband who had come to work, excited about Renata's pregnancy. When he'd known these people, he'd been obsessed with the correct paint color to stimulate intellectual development in a baby. He'd discussed the use of primary colors and repetitive shapes to promote spatial and logical thinking. His mind flashed to five fingers equally spaced and held over the primary color red.

He had to force his thoughts back to the present. "Thank you for the flowers."

Beth rested her hand against his arm, and William shied away. In the corner, Renata's dark eyes flashed with anger. Beth had touched Renata's spot, the spot where she had left her blood to soak into his flesh. William rubbed his arm, uncomfortable in this room of people who only thought they knew him.

"I'm sorry," William said when he saw Beth's face. She could order him out of this room. She had the power to keep him away from his plan, and he couldn't allow that to happen. He had to complete his task, and that meant he needed to play his part. He would pretend a contrition that he didn't feel. "She touched me here." William offered up his pain as a sacrifice.

"Oh, William." Beth moved in again, but this time she rested a dark hand on his shoulder instead.

"They should have fried that bastard," George said. He was the youngest of them, a man still interested in weightlifting and not yet interested in lowering his cholesterol.

"George!" Beth hissed the word in anger.

"They should have," William agreed before Beth could say more. "He killed Renata. He should have burned."

William's guts tightened at the thought of that kid sitting in court with his hair trimmed and his church-boy suit. If he had any feelings, he would have been too ashamed to sit in that room and allow his lawyer to play games with diagrams of blood splatter and DNA. Renata had been reduced to pieces and parts in full color pasted to poster boards and propped up for the jury. Renata herself had sat beside William, her eyes condemning her killer, and her blood dripping over the courtroom, and yet the judge had the gall to say the word "mercy" and then look at that murderer. There was no mercy in that courtroom.

"The Day of Judgment is coming, he'll burn. He'll burn in hell for what he did." George said. William nodded. He'd never had much in common with George, but now he considered the man through new eyes. Clearly George understood the enormity of the task that William had undertaken. Of course, the universe didn't actually need William; he wasn't foolish enough to assume that his participation could change the numbers of an entire universe. The universe was more powerful than a clan of scrambling, scratching manikins who crawled over the earth on wooden knees. But he wanted to be part of the turning of the wheel. He wanted his hand on the numbers.

"Let's just give William some time," Beth said, and she used her hand to guide him toward his workstation. Her glare, however, remained focused on George.

William ignored the silent contest between the two of them. He reached out and touched the cool glass surface. His numbers were all waiting for him, flashing black against gray, oblivious to the fact they were ticking off the final seconds of the universe. Computer screens answered his touch, delivering information on systems and safety protocols and porn. Porn. Clearly Jimmy had been using his computers during his leave.

The image of the woman sprawled against the white sheet became Renata. She'd laid herself out on the bed, soft music and candles and dark hair spread over the white pillow. One glass of red wine waited on the side table.

"You are so beautiful." William stood at the door of their bedroom, watching her, enthralled to her curves, her smile, her dark look that made so many silent promises.

"Yes, I am." She'd smiled wider, amused by her own cocky attitude. William smiled back.

"It's a good thing I'm smart enough to marry a good woman when I see her." William moved to the bed and sat on the edge, his fingers stroking her warm, strong leg.

"You were brilliant when you married me," she agreed.

"Where's my wine?" He leaned down and captured her lips in a quick kiss.

"That is your wine."

He'd looked at her with a confused frown. "Then where's your wine?"

"I will not be having wine tonight," she said, and she had that look in her face. Renata was a terrible poker player because her joy always leaked out of her, like sunshine slipping through the fabric of a curtain. Right now, her whole face looked backlit by joy.

"Renata?"

"I will not be having wine for about... oh, seven more months." She smiled and spread her fingers out across her stomach.

William had blinked and stared and sat with mouth agape until she'd laughed at him.

"Say something, you idiot," she'd said with a playful slap on his arm.

"You..." he'd looked from her face to that hand resting over her belly. The belly swelled, rising up and then a tiny line of red appeared, a curve to match Renata's smile. William watched while skin and muscle split. The white layers were laid out like an archeological dig, and then blood began to pour out of the wound. Her hand clawed at her stomach, as if she could hold it closed herself. Looking up, her smile had vanished, and her face was twisted by a bruised and split cheek and cut lip.

"William?" William jerked himself out of his memory and realized the illicit image was still on the screen. The woman in the picture was lighter than

Renata—her breasts were larger and had the artificial roundness of implants.

"Someone was looking up porn on the Internet," William said, his voice shaky as he tried to escape the memory. Renata smiled at him sadly from the far side of the room.

Beth sat down next to him and studied his face. People had moved. Jimmy was gone and Aizel was looking over printout instead of watching her monitor. William glanced at the computer's time stamp and realized he'd lost a couple of hours. Where?

"We are glad to have you back," Beth offered, her voice little more than a whisper. She didn't look like the sort of person to try and destroy the universe, but he knew she would try. She'd want to leave the world twisting in birth pain, without hope of giving birth to time. At one point, maybe William would have been the same, but he needed time to be reborn so that he could find Renata again. And that meant that he had to keep Beth away. William wasn't angry at her though.

"But should you be back so soon? We'd all be happy to donate a few more personal days so you can have some time off. Maybe you should spend the holidays with your parents." Beth looked at him.

William ignored the suggestion that he go to his parents' house. Their grief was only a veneer over the relief they felt at not having to smile and speak softly to a woman they'd always hated. Every time his mother tried to comfort him, William felt an almost homicidal rage. He shook his head. "I don't want to sit in the house and think about her. I'd rather be here."

Beth looked away. "Dr. Marconi said you'd feel that way. He lost his wife, too, you know." William nodded. He knew Marconi would get his own wife back along with everyone else, but that didn't erase the pain of the loss.

"I'll threaten Jimmy if he uses your terminal again." She stood and gave him a pat on the shoulder before she went back to her work station at the front of the room. The computer beeped as she logged out before heading for the door.

George looked up when Beth left the room. The door barely had time to close before he was up out of his chair. He dropped into the seat next to William's work station. "That bastard who killed Renata had no idea what a wonderful woman that little shit took away when he killed Renata. I can't believe that ass only got six years--that sentence was a joke."

"Wooden people—no emotions," William answered vaguely. The dream memory still clung to him like the blood that had dried on his arm. He remembered the nurse trying to clean him up. Renata's blood had dried so that his arm hairs were glued together with it.

"What?"

"What what?" William asked in return. He looked over and George was staring at him with either confusion or concern.

"Who's wooden?"

"I said that?" Panic clawed up through William's stomach and into his throat.

"Yeah," George leaned close, his blue eyes dancing over William's face like William was a math puzzle that he could figure out if he just applied the right formula. Maybe George would understand. William wanted someone to understand.

"The Mayans. They believed that the creator made a race of mud people and then a race of wooden people and then finally they made man."

"The Mayans?" George sounded pretty skeptical, but then George liked his Newtonian math, his weights, and very little else.

"It's..." William struggled with how much to say. He leaned close and whispered conspiratorially. "It's like we aren't real men. We're the wooden ones, the defective ones who can't feel anything. We're the manikins who the creator made, but he didn't give us hearts. How else could that boy have done that to Renata? He looked right into her eyes, he saw her pregnant stomach, and he..." William gasped for air. The world was red and five fingers pulled at him. Reaching down, he touched the wedding ring still around his finger.

"Some people just aren't wired right. They shouldn't have cut him slack, though. If he was stoned and having some sort of acid trip, that doesn't make what he did any less horrific."

William nodded--a false assurance that he had come to terms with the injustice of that boy being offered mercy when he hadn't shown Renata any. The truth was that everyone had a wooden heart. The judge had said that the baby wasn't a real person. She had hands and feet and arms and legs. She had a brain and if a surgeon had cut her out carefully, she would have cried and waved her limbs and complained about being born into the cold world. But because her lungs had never taken air, she wasn't a person.

The newspaper reporters had pressed in so close that they had scattered Renata's atoms and slipped in her blood on the steps of the courthouse. They'd trampled her as she stood with her fingers clutching their child, still in her split stomach. If they had hearts, they'd see her brown eyes staring at them in confusion, but they couldn't. They were monkeys scrambling to get him to a say a word into a microphone.

George stood up and gave him a slap on the back. "Maybe those Mayans were onto something. Some people do seem to have wood instead of beating hearts. But you have a lot of people on your side in this. Okay?"

William nodded again.

George headed back to his station, and now William focused on his numbers.

"Maybe this is not a good idea." Renata sat next to him. He didn't look at her because if he looked at her, then he would see her bleeding all over the chair.

He didn't answer her, but his fingers clicked on the keys, searching security protocols and cooling systems. If the computer thought the silo was running hot, then it disengaged standard security in order to allow unusual commands during repairs.

"I miss you," she whispered, and then her words were smoke around him as she vanished. But he would get her back.

The Gouger of Faces, the Mayans had called the one who would end the days of the manikins. The boy had gouged Renata's face, but he was a monkey, a puppet made of wood that had no more power than a fly sitting on the edge of an orchard. The real Gouger of Faces was under William's hand.

His memory skipped forward instead of skipping backwards. Winds ripped flesh from bones. Skin bubbled and blackened and rubbed off like snake's skin. But time was a circle, so he'd done all this before.

It shouldn't surprise him that he could remember what hadn't yet happened. The world would end, and the world would restart, and he would have Renata back again. He would value her more next time. He would leave his numbers and come home, and slide into the bed and just hold her as she read her books.

His memory skipped and the Gouger of Faces blew through a city, ripping out eyes so that blood tears fell. Crunching Jaguar followed, burning the flesh from the bone and devouring it with perfect mathematical precision. The splitting atom must seem godlike to people who count days with stone and stars, so William forgave the Mayans for their imperfect naming of the gods that would end the world. The Heart of Sky came with the name Hurricane blew across the world and brought darkness.

The facts were laid out so perfectly that William with all his perfect math couldn't deny the wisdom of the Mayans. He was the hand that would release the gods the Mayans had seen, and he would restart the universe.

William watched as George left for break. Jimmy and Beth were still gone. Maybe they were having sharp words about porn and use of government resources. Aizel was the only one left now. This was his best chance. He triggered the alarm and watched as the yellow lights were drowned in the red. The alarm wailed in the distance, warning the perimeter and the security, but not so loud as to distract the workers who were on the real front line. All the power of this silo ran through this room and through these numbers.

"Dr. Barros?" Aizel called out in panic. She looked around, her eyes darting from one panel to another to try and find some alarm-worthy error, but there weren't any. The numbers were perfect.

"Just take a second and read off the numbers," he ordered her calmly.

"But Beth..."

"The alarm is a lockdown. We don't have time to override and get her in here. Just read off my numbers, Aizel," William said firmly. Aizel was nearly white with fear, but she left her station and moved into one of the primary stations. In a shaking voice, she read off numbers that made no sense unless you could see William's screen. He'd opened containment, and the low levels of radiation from the old warheads were triggering alarms even though the computer firmly and erroneously insisted that the containment was secure.

Renata took a seat next to Aizel and watched her. The blood became a pool under their feet.

"William? Dr. Barros? What's going on? Where's the breech?" Beth's voice demanded his attention over the radio. William would have silenced it, only there weren't any computer protocols for that. Dr. Marconi had planned for so many emergencies, including an invasion. William triggered those commands now, and a new set of locks engaged.

"Dr. Barros? Aizel, what's going on?"

Aizel glanced over, but William focused on the perfect beauty of his numbers. It made sense for the universe to be a circle, for all things to go back to where they began. Maybe this wasn't even the beginning of the circle... maybe the translation was wrong and this was only the end of the age of the manikins and now the real men could rise from the ashes. That made William smile. He could be the father of a whole race. While a million true humans with real hearts calling him father could ease the sting of a lost daughter and a lost wife, it still didn't stop the pain.

"Dr. Barros is trying to find the containment breech." Aizel answered the radio. She was inconsequential.

"Aizel, open the doors."

Aizel stood up. She had to manually do that from the inside. Anything else would trigger even more defenses all designed by Dr. Marconi to defeat the most determined intruder.

William waited until she was in front of his station, and then he stood up and backhanded her with all his strength. He'd never hit another person with any intent to do harm. He'd never wanted to before Renata had died. Aizel's arms flailed in the air as her body turned at an impossible angle relative to the ground. Gravity took her, and she slammed into a work station. The gray glass edge was now stained with tiny drops of blood that matched the blood on the floor from Renata's eternal wounds.

"Aizel?" the radio called. William returned to his station. "Aizel?" Beth's voice was annoying him now. He flipped the speaker switch at his station.

"She's not going to answer."

"William?" Beth asked, her wooden brain obviously not understanding the simplest truths.

"Yes." His numbers finally found perfection and the locks on the missile disengaged to allow for manual inspection. The launch might be less predictable without a stable support, but William didn't care where the missile landed as much as he cared about releasing the gods and allowing the universe to tend to the rest.

"William, what are you doing?"

"Restarting the world," he answered honestly. The radio went silent for several minutes after that, and William worked with only the comforting chirp of computers and the distant wail of the alarm. They were like the tribal drums of some shaman, escorting him as he completed a holy task.

"William?" Beth sounded artificially calm. "William, explain what you mean by restarting the world."

"The world has to restart today." William knew it wasn't an explanation, but he didn't want to sully his work by explaining it in words that fit into tiny brains.

"William, is Aizel there?"

William looked over to the small pile of human on the ground. "Yes," he answered.

"Is she okay?"

"I don't know."

The radio went totally silent--the sound of background voices and the clicking of feet against tile vanished. He talked to the computer, giving it numbers for hot test firings without giving it the numbers to shut it down. Another computer chirped, asking if he truly wanted to close the missile launch doors. William smiled and undid Beth's work with a few clicks. The universe would not be cheated so easily.

The radio returned with a little click. "William, George says you were talking about wooden people today. Does that have something to do with why the world needs restarting?" He didn't answer. "William, I really want to understand. You know me; I always want to get into the middle and really understand."

Renata laughed. She was sitting on a low adobe wall outside the church, her white dress getting dirty, but she never seemed to care about that. "I can't explain God to you. God isn't a number you can put in one of your computers."

"Everything is a number," William argued. Renata was beautiful and funny and talented. She was playing Cinderella in the college musical, and William still couldn't understand what she saw in him. Oh, his mother had a comment or two about the quality of her ancestors, but William ignored that.

"Everything may have a number, but a number is not everything," she'd argued. William might have come back with an elegant mathematical formula to prove her wrong, but she was an English major, and he couldn't argue elegant numbers with her. He was limited to words.

"The universe is a mathematical construct."

She held up her hand to stop him. "Imagine," she said, the sun shining against one side of her face so that she moved her hand to shade herself from the light. "You have a plane very high up, and out of the plane, a man drops twenty nails. How many hit the earth?"

"Quantum mechanics or Newtonian physics?"

She'd smiled at his nerdy humor. "Earth logic," she countered.

"Twenty."

"If I drew a circle on the ground, what are the odds that all the nails would fall in that circle?"

"If you drew the circle here and the plane was in Argentina, I could give you those odds, but if this is a real math problem, you would have to give me velocity and wind speeds and diameters."

18

"You are such a nerd." She'd already kicked off her heels, so when she gently kicked him, her bare toes had pressed into his thigh. He often called himself a nerd, but only around other nerds. Renata was the only woman he knew who was clearly not a nerd and who could still use the word as a term of endearment.

"Now, imagine the falling nails all land in one roof, in a straight line and that the line fastens down the shingle that was there waiting for it."

"Okay, that's just not..."

"But it happened," she interrupted him. "All your numbers and science tell us how creation happened, but for all those events to happen in such a way that they create this...." She'd looked around at the wispy desert tree with the tiny leaves and the church and William standing in the sun. "It is like the nails falling in a straight line."

"What does this have to do with whether or not I have to give up Sunday morning golf for church?"

"The odds of those nails falling in a line, those are not good numbers. The odds of life developing from no life are equally bad numbers. What changed the equation?"

William stared at her, struggling to find illogic in her logic. She smiled and looked down and then frowned. Bringing her hands up, she pressed against her stomach. "William?" He reached down to touch her arm because she was on the ground now. "The baby. It hurts, William." Her voice was a hoarse whisper and her skin split under his hands, showing a gaping wound. "Dios mios. Bendita tú eres entre todas las mujeres." Blood filled it like a slow moving river, and her bare stomach was smeared with red from her hands trying to hold the two sharp edges together. Her panties were still around one ankle, but other than that, she was naked, and his fingers were red and slippery on the phone. He couldn't dial.

The universe was a circle, and he couldn't keep circling back to this failure.

"... those children. Do they deserve to die? Are you willing to kill them?"

"What?" William frowned. His numbers had changed. Someone was trying to stop him. He started typing, furiously lying to the computer as he sought to regain the ground he'd lost. He fed in a sequence of test scenarios, and then turned off the testing protocols.

"William, you're killing people."

"People die all the time," William countered.

"Talk to me about the wooden people. Who are the wooden people?" Beth asked, her voice still calm. William had to give her credit; she'd earned the promotion to head of the unit with her ability to remain calm. Atoms raged in their cages and gods howled for release, but she was still calm. A computer chirped about movement in a lateral shaft, and William vented hot steam through the tunnel. Whatever had been moving in there wasn't now.

"We're wooden people. The Mayans—the believed the second age of man was flawed. The creator had to destroy them because they had no feelings."

It took her a few minutes to answer. "I can understand why you feel that way. What happened to Renata is terrible, but hurting other people won't bring her back."

"Yes it will."

Another silence. "You have to explain the logic of that one, William. Just walk me through your numbers."

There was more movement, this time in the base of the missile silo. That was a dangerous place to be with the test engines hot and ready to fire. William prepped the order to fire.

"People are flawed. They're made of wood and have no feelings. But today is the end of this part of the universe. December 21, 2012. The day when the gods go free and restart the world. I'll see Renata again when we come around to this point in the universe on the next cycle."

"Okay, you say people have no feelings, but I've got two kids, William. You know how much I love those kids."

"No, I don't. I don't know what you feel." The logic of that felt right, and she didn't have a quick answer.

"Okay, fair enough. You don't. But William, I want you to think about Renata. I want you to think about how you felt when you married her, about how you felt when you found out she was pregnant. Do you remember how that felt?"

Renata was standing at the end of a long white aisle, walking toward him in a dress that shimmered with light. The computer beeped its warning about an intrusion into the cooling vent, and William pulled himself free of the memory that caught on his thoughts like cobwebs.

"I remember." The words were a talisman that held time together in one thread.

"You felt something. You loved her. We can't be the wooden people. You felt something for her."

William stopped and considered the logic of that. Renata watched him, curious and silent as he fed the computer new numbers. The missile chirped its complaint about firing engines when there was movement in the silo. New numbers made the computer comply. Preliminary engines fired, and now the only movement was the heating of air and the rising flames pressing against the concrete in preparation for the main engine.

"You love Renata. We can't be the wooden people!" For the first time, Beth's voice rose. "Stop the launch, William. We can't be the wooden people. You feel love."

William looked at Renata. She stood in her white dress, red dripping down from a torn belly. With her arms cradling her belly as if it was their child, she waited for him. Aizel was crumpled at the ground at her feet.

"I'm wood. I would have died with her if I had a real heart."

William typed in the final sequence of numbers and felt the building shiver with fire as the missile rose from the earth and loosed the gods on the world. There would be vengeance. Death would rain down on the world like the burning sap that Heart of Sky had sent down in the past and in the future. That moment would be ugly and hot and painted red and black, but it would pass like birth pains. The universe would restart and he would hold his Renata again, and lose her again, and find her again for all eternity. For a wooden man, that's the best he could hope for.

In a distant city with buildings stacked up like children's blocks and a river meandering through the steel and smog, the wind ripped through the skyscrapers, shattering glass and stripping flesh from bones. Eyes turned up to watch with curiosity were gouged out by radiation, and people fell to the ground screaming. Bits of city rose high into the air and fell from the sky, bringing hot anger. Vengeance rode the air as the world blossomed with heat and darkness rose with the dirt and the ash of millions, and the age of man ended in Hurricane winds.

2012AD

The Night of the Fifth Sun

By N. E. Chenier

Muan, the chthonic raven, came screeching into the Assembly. He grumbled around a beakful of coiled fetuses that his lord had been delayed and, thus, would be late. Again.

The Assembly roiled.

"Au Puch!" Chac roared the name of the tardy underworld god. The lights flickered. Chac's wings concussed, and fields of corn crop the size of Iowa withered into brown husks.

Ixtab yanked at the rope around her neck so that her eyes bulged in their sockets until red tears scoured her face and blood rained from the clouds over Central America. "Some things never change," she rasped.

The solar Ahaw Kin shook his golden feather-maned head. "Of all days," he growled. His displeasure set off wildfires in Southern California and across most of Peru.

Ah Puch late. The Assembly could hardly get much accomplished before the Underworld god made his appearance.

The relative youngster of the gathering, Yumil Kaxob, a grain god, emerged from his pouting over the lost corn. He'd helped coax the crops into fruition so it was his right to destroy them--not Chac's. His indignation didn't last long. There was too much to look forward to with the immanent rollover--Yumil's first--and plenty more crops to blast. Yumil had been scanning the arena intently before the messenger demon Muan started drooling fetal tissue all over the display. "Didn't they have the support pyramids up earlier?" he asked, not finding them where he thought he'd seen them before.

IxChel had on her most garish robe: rainbows carved stark, harsh streaks around her torso. She gestured to a spot in the White Realms of the north, where much activity buzzed as the cycle drew toward its end. "They used to be here," she said.

Old Votan grinned his black teeth. "Not anymore!" he sang with a voice like war drums. He beat his fists together until tar ran from the wounds over his knuckles.

"Twelve solar years ago," Ixtab gurgled. Lady Suicide knew. She had been there with Votan. They had been busy through the entire round, among those who had not gone into the Long Sleep. How could they? The humans kept them constantly invoked. Ah Puch, being the third, kept his own time and never slept. "It wouldn't have sustained them anyway."

If Kukulcan, preeminent among the Assembly, was jealous of the attention the mortal creatures universally awarded the trio, he didn't show it. The serpentine lightning god had long since earned his respect--and his rest. But now the god was refreshed, ready. Blue lightning lanced over his scaly plumage and across spectral wings. Over the congregation, his great head loomed on massive coils--massive even compared with the sun god, Ahaw Kin. "No, it wouldn't have," he hissed without anger. "That they were removed is merely a sign of the insupportable state of Creation." His obsidian gaze found Huichaana and her husband lurking in the shadowy terraces about the perimeter with the congregation of the lesser gods. "I'm sorry, Huichaana."

The glistening goddess shrugged and shook her head. Stony stoicism jaded her expression. Beside her--yet keeping an obvious space between them--her husband Cozaana was not as stoic. The green god wept for the life he and his wife had created for this, the fourth world. Huichaana had created the humans while he had worked on everything else: plant and animal life. His part of the project was blameless.

Au Puch appeared among the company in his violent Kam-aspect, the skull visage burning red as an infected wound. Charred bones clattered together in his matted hair.

"At last," spat Ahaw Kin, fangs like bloody pillars bared at the skeletal god. "Let's get to it."

* * *

Huichanna wasn't part of the clean up crew, but she descended anyway to move among the creatures of her design. Kukulcan, patronizing in his largess, pretended not to notice. Let the Great Serpent think he was being indulgent; she'd earned the right to take a last stroll. Besides, there was only so much of

Cozanna's sniveling she could stand. While the others plotted over the spots already volatilized by the war god Voltan, Huichanna bent her attention to quieter realms.

A long sleep had passed since she'd come to witness the animated beings of her devising. And now, with the end of their day fast approaching, Huichanna regretted not having come to see them sooner. She delighted in their variety, the divergent paths a single design could take. She let herself be drawn by flares of emotion, down into their dwelling places.

* * *

In the yellow kitchen of their mother's house, Herman tried to make his sister listen to reason. Marie had that infuriating way about her that made her appear to be the reasonable one even when he was laying out cold hard facts. He presented her with scientific evidence only to have her sigh heavily, as if Herman was still ten years old and it fell upon her shoulders to show him truth.

Herman resisted the pigeonhole of excitable kid brother to her elder-sibling omniscience. The facts were on his side, he told himself.

"We are not perpendicular to the galactic plane, Herman," she said, a smile tugging at the corners of her lips as if she were waiting for him to deliver the punch line, for surely he couldn't believe anything so ridiculous.

He had her this time. He waved her onto the back porch. "There!" he said, more loudly than he had intended.

Marie shook her head. "Hermie?"

Tracing the smear of the Milky Way in the sky with his hand, Herman asked, "What does that tell you?"

"That in summer we're on the side of the sun that's closest to the galaxy's center?"

Why was she being so obtuse? He sliced the sky again with his hand. "Up and down. Up and down. See?"

Her eyebrows went up, crinkling deep ridges into her forehead.

Before he could shout in exasperation, he took a deep breath. He was right this time. There was no need to get excited. Herman mustered his calm. "It's sideways."

Then, she did it. She laughed, that derisive, superior laugh, the one that pulled him back into gawky adolescence. "Oh, Herman, it's up and down because we are on the side of a sphere." She went back into the kitchen, fetched a plastic apple and a banana from the corningware bowl on the table. "The sun traces the same pattern in the sky as the Milky Way. They pretty much share the same plane." She tried to illustrate with the banana, but Herman knew she didn't really know what she was talking about. The astronomer on-line had the charts and everything to prove it.

Marie finally stopped gesturing with the plastic fruit. Her shoulders sagged. "Okay, Herman, okay. What significance does the Milky Way being 'sideways' to us have?"

He hesitated, waiting for that mocking grin, but her expression remained sober, so he took the wobbly chair across from her. "Okay, see, it means we weren't originally from this galaxy. We're just coming into it."

Her eyebrows rode high on her forehead, but had yet to reach mocking height. "And this has something to do with the Mayan calendar?"

"Well, as you know, the long count calendar finishes on the solstice in 2012, and according to the astronomers, that's when our solar system will finally line up with the rest of the galaxy. We'll be home and so the new era can begin." It held perfect symmetry for him. All the problems, turmoil of the world could be traced by humanity's unsatisfied longing to find and define home and family. All the greed and land-grubbing and rabid insistence on ownership, all that garbage in the Middle East--it came from not really having a place to belong, from being adrift, an emotional response to the conflicting gravitational lines.

Marie's eyes softened. "Home," she said significantly and for a moment he thought she understood. She cast her gaze around the kitchen, the curling pizza coupons under fridge magnets, the dusty rank and file of bottles yet to make it to recycling. "It never really has been, has it?"

His shoulders sagged. "This isn't about this damn house." He pitched his voice low so his mother in the den wouldn't hear above the volume of the "Caressed by a Guardian" marathon.

Those too insecure to throw off the violence, too inured to war to recognize they had arrived, would perish in the new era. They would never be at *Home* in the universe, so when the rollover occurred, they would be out with the old.

"Well," Marie said, as if conceding, but actually conceding nothing, "you're not alone in your ideology."

She stretched and cricked her neck, prelude to motion. She never could sit still for more than a few minutes at a time. "And all this is why you're holing up in the Rockies next winter?" She stood and reached for her shoulder bag.

Mom must have told her. His friend Geoffrey had a place up there which he'd outfitted with a bomb shelter back during the Y2K thing.

"It's best to be away from the cities," he admitted, half-hoping she would heed his advice, half-hoping she wouldn't and see for herself how right he was.

"For how long, exactly?" The chipper tone told him she was humoring him again.

He shrugged. Marie was a striver. As a kid she was always one-upping him, her classmates, her co-workers. In the 13th Baktun, it landed her a windowed office in a Chicago skyscraper. Herman wondered if her nature would be able to set aside its ceaseless ambition enough to survive into the 14th.

In the way she dismissed what was right in front of her, he doubted it.

* * *

Huichanna couldn't help but suffer fondness for the creature, his blindness coupled with accidental insight. Remorse squashed the flutter of mirth. She couldn't bear that all his kind would be eradicated by Kukulcan and the rest of the Assembly—and there was no countering the determination of the lightning god on this point, nor the glee of the others. Huichanna brooded over the quibbling human siblings. She had no allies.

Then again, she might have one.

* * *

The rainbow goddess, IxChel, ornamented the swirling clouds with brilliant color, such a wild mix they ended up roiling into angry bruises, reflecting her own discontent.

IxChel suffered from sentimentality. It was silly, she told herself as she pushed through the glass pane into the building. She was sorry to see the fourth world go. It had held such promise. But, the others were right: it had turned into a royal mess by the end.

She got pulled to the cities first. The metropolis had dazzled her once: how inventive the little creatures are! The neon tangles and rainbow fires that burned all night delighted her. But as she moved through the next and the next, the differences blurred into monotony.

The hospital was like the last thousand she had passed through, her bare feet padding through cold sterile halls, up to the seventh floor. The ward was full. Women with swelling bellies slept on cots that had been drawn into the waiting rooms. Women seeking refuge and care for the new lives stirring within them.

The first human world—in the age of the Second Sun--had been destroyed because the gods got scared. Their creations had been as powerful as their makers and lost their humility just as fast as they learned how to use their powers.

IxChel touched a sweating brow. With her other hand, she drew two fingers across the crest of a round abdomen. The young woman's eyelids fluttered, and she moaned in her sleep. A slow stain soaked the pillow tucked between her legs. The woman shuddered, but she didn't wake.

The second human world had them of wood, the third of stone, but both amounted to little more than stupid puppets, and the gods quickly bored of them. This time seemed the perfect compromise. Huichaana had not only chosen clay, but had labored to infuse them with individual consciousness, and before his slumber, Kukulcan had given them a code of law. Little good it did them.

The goddess moved to the next woman and again, two fingers untied the string of fertility from the sleeper. Crimson burst at the hem of the white hospital gown. One by one, IxChel emptied their wombs.

Why couldn't they get the humans right? Her gentle sorrow rained over the city in her wake.

* * *

Ixtab, Lady of the Martyrs, was patient. She strode across the desert battlefields, dragging the loose end of her noose over the pitted earth in the wake of the elder Votan. Torsos rent of their limbs, collapsed under her bloated feet. The war god Votan had it easy. Age had done nothing to rob him of his vitality, not with all the worship feeding him constantly. It paid to be a war god under the Fifth Sun.

Votan basked in the devotion coming from temples in the new North.

"Prince of peace!" he guffawed, thumping the plateau of his chest. "They love me!" He swelled, bloated with their prayers. Prayers for victory, prayers for death and prayers for revenge. If the underworld god Ah Puch weren't so otherwise preoccupied, he'd be glutting himself at their altars too.

Ixtab sipped gently from the edges of the sacrifices to Votan, coiled her rope around the few that stumbled her way. She could afford patience. Much more of Votan's flock would be delivered to her before the turnover was complete.

The dust billowed around her. Smoke lowered the night sky and glowed the color of an irradiated corpse. Flashes of rocket fire punctuated the ongoing sentence of battle. The trio had been spending a lot of time here: old hatreds cloaked in religious robes, unchecked oppression. The gods didn't need to be called by name to respond to the beacons.

One such beacon called Ixtab into the passenger seat of a rickety van as a youth steered past a checkpoint.

* * *

The dust smeared across the windshield glared in the afternoon sun. The passenger door was held closed by a belt looped to the passenger seat. She could see the gritty road through the rust holes at her feet.

Ixtab just loved these boys, so fresh, so eager to embrace her shriveled breasts. In these last days, she multiplied herself to attend every one of them. She didn't recognize the Name quivering on his lips, though. Votan by another name, she supposed.

Ari was only half aware of her, hopped up on the importance and finality of his mission - *the mission*. The lot had fallen to him. His hands fluttered on the wheel.

The recent chaos of the weather provided the perfect cover. Earthquakes had toppled the buildings, the walls, fractured the security of the cities. Little remained standing of Ari's neighborhood. Sand storms continued to rear out of the desert like tidal waves, flinging dust with such ferocity it could strip a man of his armor in five minutes and down to his skeleton in another two. The first one had reduced his own uncle to a pile of scoured bone. The generals were calling it proof of divine wrath, struggle of good and evil coming to a head. The very land was rearing up to eat the host of invading demons. As he was told again and again, Ari was a warrior of God.

The soldiers at the checkpoint weren't letting any new faces through, but Ari had been running innocuous deliveries since before he could drive. He was familiar, harmless little Ari. He nodded to Mr. Yosef and Mr. Samuel, dutifully showed his transit permits, edges ragged from repeated passing between incautious fingers. No need for words. It had been a tense week. He schooled his expression into sympathy. The bomb breathed beneath him.

If he weren't always the most vehement of soldiers, he played that part now. There had not been much else for him to do. Most of his classmates had turned to the resistance after the school had been bombed. He had been just a boy, the oldest of four children, and the only hope for a widowed mother. The resistance offered a promise of glory and, of course, money – money for a young man with a struggling family.

They ate well in the occupied city. The quake and storms barely affected business within the security zone. The generals would have preferred him to steer into the glitzy shopping district, but his dilapidated vehicle would be prevented from entering the new quarter. That was fine. They had a more accessible target for him.

At the restaurant attached to an international hotel, the lunch crowd lounged on clean patios, the food and drink flowing freely for them. The cost of one meal could have fed an extended family for a month.

He could sense the spirit next to him. Was it because he was so close to death that he earned the guidance of an angelic messenger? When the orders had come, Ari hadn't felt at all chosen by god, no matter what the other cadets said. The relief in their eyes told a different story: *thank god it's not me.* It gave Ari a measure of comfort finally to get tangible divine approval.

Ixtab stifled a giggle by tightening her noose.

The gates of heaven opened to receive him like a lover.

He twisted the wheel, slammed the gas pedal. The engine roared and wheezed, but the truck jolted over the curb, lunged at the wrought iron encircling the patio. Diners dove out of the way of the wheels. The steering wheel was useless as the truck bounced through the grate, veered across the patio, scattering tables, wine glasses, heaping plates.

The cab slammed into the picture window and lurched to a halt. Ari scrabbled behind his calves for the trigger. Ixtab bent the dangling piece into his hands. It was the least she could do.

Lodged half in the restaurant, half still on the patio, Ari forced his eyes open, to meet his god unbowed.

Fire bloomed, rolled in two directions, petals unfurling into the sky, petals thrusting into the interior to tangle with gas stoves and chemically treated hairdos.

The heavenly creature leaned in. Wide, lovely eyes like a gazelle's. The prophets were telling the truth--not that he doubted them--when they said beautiful virgins were supposed to welcome martyrs. She held out her arms to the blackened body twisted upside down in the cab. He responded without thinking.

"Are we going to Beulah?" he asked. He was surprised to find desire still in tact.

He tried to reach for her, but the remains of the vehicle crushed his arms.

He frowned. Surely, he was dead, the black thing a husk and his spirit set free to cavort in the vale of eternal and varied beauty. Ari looked to her for an explanation.

Very close now. A whiff of sweetness tickled his nose. Sweet decay.

The hazy visage encompassing the wide-set eyes resolved into a landscape of angry purple. The cloying sweetness engulfed him in hot corrosion. He gagged.

"How can you enter Beulah with no legs?" the blistered lips asked.

This was no virgin. A demon. How was it possible? Hadn't he earned a privileged place in the afterlife?

He slithered from the wreckage. No pain, but he flopped like a beached fish, no control over his body. Ripped flesh crisscrossed his shredded shirt. His legs ended at the knees in charred tatters. Why was his soul in this shape? Why couldn't he shuck this broken husk? He looked back at the cab, the activity swarmed around it, and he could see a charred skeleton twisted in the metal. Blood bubbled out his throat as he struggled to voice his disbelief.

"There's always room in Ah Puch's domain," the demon said. The language was unfamiliar but resolved itself in Ari's head. What had he to do with demons? It was a mistake. Another test?

A cold tendril slithered around Ari's neck. He clawed at it with fingers of blackened bone.

"Don't know about any virgins, though. You'll have to ask around." The demon hauled on the rope and lifted him off the ground.

IxTab swung Ari's noose like a pendulum until she got enough momentum to complete a circle. She whirled the boy over her head like a lasso, then released him. He streaked like a comet against the night. Her aim was perfect.

She was sure going to miss the antics of the fourth human world.

* * *

Chac sent the rain over the prairies. He sank his broken fangs into the thunderheads. Black tears poured like tar around his crooked snout into the tumescent clouds. Sparks flared from his serrated talons.

Across the countryside, people rushed from their farmhouses. Parched from long drought, they threw their arms wide as if to embrace the deluge. The Benson family laughed and hugged each other, their relief commingling with the dance of raindrops on their faces. The violet lightning that cracked across the black clouds didn't distract them from their euphoria.

Then Kaitlin, the youngest, started screaming. She balled her fists into her eyes and wailed. Randal Benson knelt next to his daughter, thinking to rid the child of a fleck of dust from her eye when he too felt the sting. Steam rose from his skin.

It wasn't cold enough for steam.

Randal wrapped his bare arms around his wailing child, tried to shield her with his body.

"Get them inside!" he yelled at his wife. Cathy, spurred by the panic in his voice, lunged toward Mikey, who started his own keening cry.

Randal couldn't get to the house fast enough. The burn blanched over his exposed skin, blisters swelled before his eyes and burst. The skin flayed away to expose craters of criss-crossing veins. "David!" he choked through swelling lips. "Oh God, hurry!" He sagged inside the hall.

His older boy hunched into a protective ball. The fabric across the back of T-shirt smoked. "Daddy?" David whimpered, rubbing his arms. His skin came off like sleeves. His screams died before they could explode from his throat. A jagged gurgle broke from the molten mess of his face.

Cathy collapsed before she made it under the eaves. Her hair peeled off with the flesh of the scalp revealing a pink cap that pitted under the acid rain. Ragged hands shoved Mikey ahead of her, but the boy fared no better. His squalls echoed in Randal's ears.

This can't be happening, he thought wildly. Doomsday's not real. Eschatological fairy tales...

Kaitlin wasn't breathing. The child stared at the ceiling with blanched eyeballs. The acid still worked at the flesh of his daughter's face like a frenetic archaeologist picking away bits of dried mud from a fossil bone.

The stench of sour meat clogged his breath. The house groaned and snapped around him. Where was the rapture?

With the last of his strength, Randal crawled to the bathroom, dragging a fat slug-trail of gore behind him. He made it to the sink, but the water he dowsed himself with pulled the rest of the flesh from his forearms--and did nothing to neutralize the last rain of the thirteenth Baktun.

Ah Puch, fierce in his red-skull Kam-aspect, clapped Chac on his broad shoulder. Purple electricity launched from the contact and carved a smoking gorge in the earth's crust. "Impressive," Ah Puch said through the wind chimes of his teeth.

Ah Puch collected the steaming bones that littered the prairies, plucked them out of the wreckage of crumbling structures. Three ribs from Cathy's corpse joined the collection tied into Ah Puch's locks, a femur from little Mikey rattled with the others around his neck, a length of Randal's spine made it with the thousands dangling from the death god's waist.

Ah Puch preferred Chac's expediency to Votan's messily drawn out destruction, especially this time around. The Kam part of him liked the violence

40

of the lightning god's choice, and the Underworld part of him approved of the simplicity of dissolution. The Assembly had a lot of ground to cover, more than ever.

* * *

While Kukulcan remained in the Upper Realms beyond, the gods amassed for their final descent into their wasted creation. Ahaw Kin, the shape-shifting solar god, took the vanguard position. His aura spread before him, illuminated by the veil of the material world. What yet survived of Creation beheld. The tides of human hopes and fears eddied around the solar deity's manifestation. The hopeful knelt before him with the word *Messiah* shuddering from their lips. The fearful fled and called him names usually reserved for Ah Puch.

With the crops and storehouses decimated, Yumil Kaxob got permission from the solar god, Ahaw Kin, to help him gather up the human harvest. The youthful god fanned out along the electrical currents that knit together far-flung communities. He crept into their separate residences and savored every sweep of his sickle.

At times, he found himself shored up at odd nodes. He pushed at one node and found himself running up against IxChel.

"You're still working here?" the youth blurted then hastily checked his insolence. The elder goddess turned her diamond gaze on him and he flushed.

"It's all right, Yumil Kaxob," she said, and peace settled over him. "I shall take care of these."

"Yes, Mistress," Yumil replied. He diverted his course along another fork. By the time he emerged at a new residence, where a woman sat entranced before the beaming image of Ahaw Kin, he'd completely forgotten his encounter with the rainbow goddess.

The woman was ripe for the harvest. Yumil could have taken her in a twinkling, but he wanted to give finesse to each ending. After all, who knew when he'd ever get a chance to reap humans again?

Barbara couldn't believe her eyes--no that's not true, of course she believed; she'd been looking forward to this very moment since Y2K. And how enormously amazing it was to be alive to witness the coming of the Lord. The hosts made their appearances in foreign lands: Egypt, India, Africa, and the closest in Central America. She yearned to go there and bear witness in person, but she'd just have to settle for satellite broadcasts in HD.

Jeremy'd be home any minute now and she would show him. Maybe now her son would wake up to reality. He wouldn't be able to sneer and throw convoluted arguments against what her heart had known since before she could talk. Every channel, even the shopping channel, confirmed the *Truth*.

Coming in live from Ecuador, the Messiah's descent was exactly what she'd expected. He came from the clouds on golden rays with so much brilliance that the exact details of his holy visage melded together. A host of angels framed that mighty presence, vast wings of heavenly glory stirred up the desert sands.

Yumil twined around the portals of her senses. It was a simple thing to graft a thought to a perception, an emotion to an idea.

Barbara heard her son come in. Jeremy halted in the doorway, instantly taken by what was on the screen.

"Isn't it beautiful?" she murmured. It was. So beautiful there was no need to point out that the faith had been right all along.

"Mom?" His teenager's voice quavered with all the vulnerability of a babe in arms. Barbara's heart would have swelled were it not already filled to the brim with bliss. She hadn't had to say a word. Jeremy was back in the fold.

"It's going to be okay," she said. Barbara gestured to the space next to her on the couch.

The strangled sound behind her tore her attention away from the broadcast. Jeremy's face was a mask of horror. His mouth worked and he shook his head.

"Sweetheart." Barbara was up and caught her son under his shoulders just before his gangly legs buckled under him. She stroked his hair, almost as she had when he was in kindergarten, except his hair wasn't black and stiff then. "Don't be afraid," she said. "It's not too late. Just open your heart."

He focused on his mother as if she were a stranger. "To that?" he asked incredulously.

Panic shivered in her throat. How hardened his heart was! "Jeremy," she said, summoning severity born of fear. "Do not deny this revelation. Repent and be saved before it's too late."

"Mom, what do you see on the screen right now?" Jeremy asked.

"Oh," she breathed. "The coming of the Lord." She focused on the glow swimming about the central figure. "Angels and endless light."

"That's not god."

She opened her mouth to scold him, but changed her mind. Her heart cringed. She didn't want to know, but she asked anyway, "What do you see?"

"Satan," he said. "Exactly like what they try to scare you with." He pressed a finger to the screen and traced an arc of gold light. "Here, a smoking pit. Can't you see it?" He turned up the volume.

The commentary blared out in turmoil, anchors shouting over each other. My god... evil forces... alien invasion... savior... anti-Christ... end times... Ragnarok...

As she heard, the image, that glorious image, flickered, faltered. She saw scales, lightning, and then the glory was restored. But it didn't feel like the same glory; it was tainted.

"What does it mean?" she demanded, angry now. The woman didn't apprehend any external interference; the parent plant recognized the graft as part of herself. Doubt tainted everything - Jeremy's doubt.

"It has to be some kind of trick," Jeremy said, his curiosity overriding his fear. "Mass hallucination maybe." He stood up, shook his head and pinched himself on the arm in an effort to test his senses.

An action grafted to an idea. Barbara advanced on her son, a rose quartz angel statue in her hand. It flew of its own accord, lifting her hands over her head. She watched it plummet with her hands down onto the back of Jeremy's skull, felt its base sink too far into his hair. A grunt escaped him, and Barbara imagined she heard her son's repentance in it.

Doubt dissipated with a ragged breath. Barbara muted the TV and beheld the Lord in full glory.

Content with the one soul, Yumil felt
magnanimous enough to leave the woman for Ixtab.

* * *

To some, Ahaw Kin appeared as a white-
bearded king, others saw a great serpent, others cheered
on a winged warrior. There were those who saw him
descend from the heavens and others who swore he
rose from a smoking pit. Some thought it was his first
visit, and others thought it was his return. The gods
attending him were eight armed angels riding horses,
wielding swords and breathing fire.

And before them, the faithful and the fearful
were uniformly annihilated.

* * *

"It is done," Kukulcan said wearily. He reclined
into the loops of his feathered coils. Wings that could
extend from horizon to horizon drooped at his sides.
Ah Puch nodded, Votan grunted, each grimly satisfied
with his work. A flushed Ixtab twirled her noose
between her palms and sighed.

The gods lolled, drunken with the released
energy of destruction. Even now, that energy gathered
like a slow storm. It drew itself languidly within each
of them, a contraction before the next World Age. A
world, Kukulcan promised himself, that would be
absent of humans.

In the tiered shadows Cozaana poked his wife.
He started to gesture to the arena, but Huichaana
pursed her lips and gave the tiniest shake of her stony
head. His eyes lit up.

Aware of the exchange, IxChel stifled a smile behind a length of rainbow silk. Over the blasted land, IxChel had drawn dull shrouds across several mountain ranges. Shrouds for enwrapping a deceased world.

Yet, if one were particularly vigilant, one might spot the scattered sparks hidden beneath her veils: one here in the White North, one there in the Red East, another tucked away in the Yellow South, maybe a couple in the Black West. IxChel searched the weary Assembly to see if any of the others suspected what she and Huicaana had secreted away. She relaxed when, at last, Ahaw Kin withdrew the remnants of his power from the world and fell into slumber. Done was done.

IxChel wondered how the remnants might fare through the night before the Sixth Sun rose. She was optimistic. If anything could be said about the clay-beings, they were a versatile race.

* * *

The air scoured into his lungs like steel wool. Herman panicked, almost swung the vault door shut again, before he realized that he was merely reacting to its freshness. He stood on the threshold, shivering. It hadn't even been a year and stepping outside was like stepping into vacuum space.

He'd been alone for almost all that time. Geoffrey had disappeared in early January after a month of fretting about his ex-wife and son, neither of whom had followed them into the mountains.

The bunker had been supplied for the whole family, but it had ended up down to Geoffrey and

Herman and then, just Herman. The long months alone, he was grateful for the library of TV games that had been meant to lure and preoccupy Jeff, Jr.

Herman shivered all over. The summer night was cool, but that probably didn't mean anything at his altitude. His vision blurred the middle distances, darkness blotted the rest. He moved around to the front of the house.

From the front door, the land sloped away and gave an open view of the sky. The stars around Sagittarius took their time coming into focus. The fuzzy strip of stars canted upward toward the left.

"God damnit!" Herman cursed through his teeth. Nothing had changed. He wasn't home yet.

2012AD

The Finality

By Steven Southard

December 21, 2011:

Books written in five languages crammed the shelves of the small office. A cluttered desk stood near the only window, filled with student's theses, a computer, and a globe of Jupiter. The room's only occupant sat in a tall chair before a blackboard, scribbling on it with a small nub of chalk. She wore a wine-colored sari from which her bare feet dangled. Her gray hair hung down, but many strands stuck out at odd angles, giving the appearance of a dusty halo when the sunlight from the window hit them. The eighty-two year old woman stopped with a shudder, dropped her chalk, and stared in apparent horror at the final equation.

"Oh, no," she said.

***

March 20, 2012:

"Good afternoon, I'm CNN Science Correspondent Blake Denton. I'm joined here in our

Washington studio by Dr. Anusha Bharatee…Bharateeyanakshatra. I'm sorry, Dr., did I pronounce that correctly?"

"Yes, Mr. Denton, but just call me Dr. Anu." Anusha wondered what Denton had been told about her theory and what tone he would strike for the interview.

"Thank you," he seemed a little relieved at not having to say her full name as he turned to the camera. "Dr. Anu is the senior professor at the Inter-University for Astronomy and Astrophysics in Pune, India. Today she astounded the International Cosmology Conference, meeting here in Washington this week. Dr., just what is your hypothesis?"

"Simply stated, my calculations show that time is running out, Mr. Denton."

"The end of the world?" His expression seemed earnest, so Anusha hoped he would treat her seriously.

Just to the right of the camera in front of her sat a monitor, on which she could see what the audience did. Beneath her image ran a text banner: "Scientist predicts end of world." She hoped that the American audience would not regard her as a kook.

"I wish it were that simple, and that localized," she said. "In such a case, a few people could escape our planet and survive. No, I am talking about the end of time itself."

"The end of time. I don't understand."

"My calculations reveal that, just as the laws of our universe emerged with the Big Bang 13.7 billion years ago, those same laws will cease to apply on a certain date in our future. Those laws are the fabric, the framework, of the universe, and they include the structure of time itself."

"You'll forgive me for being a bit skeptical—"

"I *expect* you to be skeptical, Mr. Denton. That is how science works."

"Of course, doctor. But the end of time? Have you determined when—what date that is?"

Anusha noted that the scrolling banner on the monitor had been changed to read, "Indian physicist says Time itself ending."

"Please understand," she began," that I am interpolating based on astronomical observations of the farthest edge of the known universe, analyzing radiated energy from just after the Big Bang, so there is some uncertainty about the date. Pending further refinements, I'd say the last day will occur sometime in December."

"Of this year, you mean?"

"Indeed," she said softly.

"Are you aware, Dr. Anu, of the fact that the 21st of December is the last day of the ancient Mayan calendar, and that some people have claimed that the Mayans already foresaw the end of the world on that day?"

Anusha gave a dismissive wave of her hand. "Yes, I've been told of this, Mr. Denton. Let me assure you, it can be nothing more than coincidence. My analysis is based on complex mathematics as well as precise astronomical observations of the red shift made by orbiting telescopes, cosmic microwave background radiation measurements made by the Planck Satellite, and initial data from the Ice Cube Neutrino Detector. The stone age Mayan people lacked both the knowledge and the technology to make, let alone understand, my findings."

"I see," he said. Then he shook his head. "The end of time. I'm having trouble coming to grips with that concept, Dr. Anu, as I'm sure many in our audience will. I mean, time goes infinitely far into the future. I can name future dates past December, like January of 2013."

"You could, but such dates are based on an incomplete understanding of physical laws. It would be much the same as speaking of times prior to the Big Bang, or speeds faster than light. Such concepts can be imagined, but they have no physical meaning in our universe."

"Dr. Anu, could you be wrong about this? I mean, is it possible that your calculations--?"

Anusha had heard this question from many people, all trying to deny the end, searching for any way out. She bent toward him slightly. "Indeed, I hope I am wrong, Mr. Denton. Nothing would please me more than to wake up next January with nothing ruined but my reputation and career."

"How are other scientists reacting to your theory? We've always been assured that the Earth and the universe have billions of more years to go."

She recognized this appeal to other authorities as a standard response as well--grasping at any straw. "Many cosmologists and astrophysicists have confirmed my findings. Some tell me they can find nothing wrong with my analysis, but still reject my conclusion. Others have told me that they simply refuse to examine my equations at all. But nobody has yet found an error in my work--unfortunately." The monitor's scrolling banner now read, "PhD says future ends this December."

Denton faced the camera. "For those wishing to check Dr. Anu's calculations, we've linked to her scientific papers on the CNN website, and we'll be displaying her University's e-mail address on the screen shortly," Denton said. Then he went on. "Dr. Anu, I have to ask, will we be seeing any signs of this end coming before it happens – floods, earthquakes, comets? It just doesn't feel like we're running out of months."

"I agree that this all may be difficult to accept," Anusha said, "especially since there are, as yet, no obvious signs. Moreover, the equations suggest only that the collapse of the laws of physics will occur quite late and quite suddenly, within a few microseconds of the end. Humans will, of course, not sense this collapse."

She saw in his face the look that she'd seen so often recently as people absorbed the information, the momentary stunned horror as the inevitability sank in. "When this collapse, this ending occurs, will everything just freeze? I mean, will atoms stop moving? Will light waves stop?"

Anusha paused, unable to come up with words to describe the physics in any understandable way. "It is useless to contemplate what the universe will look like after the end, since there simply is no 'after.' Time will cease to pass. Events will not occur."

Denton put a hand to his chin and tapped one finger against his upper lip. Then he seemed struck by a thought. "Dr. Anu, humanity has overcome difficulties before – ice ages, plagues – can we find some way out of this, or a way to delay it by several thousand years?"

Anusha looked at the screen and saw the banner, "Physicist says end to come without warning."

She kept her face expressionless. "It is true that our species has been remarkably adaptive, very clever at resolving challenges. While it is possible that we might find a way to prevent the end from coming, I think it's important to be realistic. This fate threatens the entire universe, Mr. Denton. It's on a scale much vaster than any problem we've solved before."

"One last question, Dr. Anu, since we're running out of ti-- I mean, we have just thirty seconds left in this news segment. Aside from checking your analysis for mistakes and working on a possible remedy, what should people do? How should they behave in the nine months remaining?"

Anusha paused as she realized that her response to this question, more than any other, might have the most significant consequences. "Behavioral Psychology is not my field, but it seems to me that-- since I may be wrong--it is best for people to go on as they would normally. I hope that people would do that."

"Ladies and gentlemen," Denton faced the camera with a sober expression, "We've all seen and heard of people predicting the end of the world, and they've always turned out to be wrong; the world kept going. But Dr. Anu is a leading expert in cosmology, the Big Bang, and the physics of time. Like many of you, I may not understand the mathematics behind her theory, but we must take this warning seriously."

***

June 20, 2012:

Anusha sat in a comfortable chair in an office within the Museo Nacional de Antropología in Mexico City. The office belonged to Dr. Luiz Canche, a Mexican expert on Mesoamerican language and culture. She looked around at the shelves packed with books, the framed photographs of Mayan architecture, and the replicas of Mayan statues. In one corner, strangely, a Mayan dagger had been thrust into the wall. She saw a chalkboard filled with symbols in an ancient language, and smiled to think how similar it looked to her own office blackboard. On another wall hung a large circular representation of the Mayan calendar.

"The Mayans thought in terms of cycles—even their calendar is a circle," Luiz said in Spanish, setting his iced tea on a coaster. "No ultimate beginnings and no ultimate endings." Too few strands of his black hair tried to cover his balding scalp. He wore glasses with black plastic frames. His open-necked white cotton shirt and khaki pants looked rumpled. Luiz's black mustache stretched out when he smiled. A lot fewer people are smiling as we get closer to The Finality, Anusha thought.

Anusha nodded at him, even though the Mayan system contrasted with the mathematics she used. The evidence of the stars had led her to the discovery that there were no infinities. Everything had limits, including time and space. The Finitism school of mathematics championed by Leopold Kronecker and Thoralf Skolem had been proven correct by astronomical observation.

Virtually all reputable scientists had by then come to agree with Anusha's calculations regarding the end of time. She had followed with interest the media's struggle to find a catch-phrase to describe the coming phenomenon, including the Big Stop, the TimeFreeze, and the Endgame, but they had settled on 'The Finality.'

"In fact, their calendar contained a number of intermeshing circles," Luiz went on, "and periodically two or more cycles would end on the same day and the Mayans would perform ceremonies and celebrate the start of a new cycle. While it is true that their Long Count calendar covers a span of 5126 years, and also true that that cycle ends this coming December, it is not true," Luiz emphasized by raising an index finger with an air of one who has been debunking the same myth for years, "that they believed the world would end at that time. I think that they would look upon it as we do the New Year holiday, nothing more."

Luiz had contacted her just after her appearance on CNN. He'd wanted to talk to her about the odd coincidence of dates between her end-of-time theory and the Mayan calendar predictions. After ignoring his first five phone messages, e-mails, and letters, she had assured him that it was nothing more than a strange quirk; no connection was possible.

Still, as she refined her calculations and narrowed down her predictions, the same date of December 21, 2012 emerged. She started wondering about the Mayans, and whether something could explain the improbable matching of two predictions— one based on primitive astronomy and instruments of wood and stone, and the other on digital computers and orbiting telescopes. The mystery of it finally intrigued her, so she had decided to leave India for a few days and study the Mayans with Luiz. She had arrived in Mexico City only the day before.

Anusha's eyes wandered back to the corner of the office where a dagger—evidently of Mayan design—stuck horizontally into a piece of paper tacked to the wall. On the paper, a picture depicted a man with dark features who sat wearing a brown robe with a white collar. His mouth was expressionless and his eyes were downcast, as if he was reading or in deep contemplation. The knife pierced the center of his chest. "Who is that?" she asked.

Luiz followed her gaze. "Diego de Landa," he said with a scowl, "and I hope he rots forever in the foulest pit of Hell."

"What has he done to you?" Anusha wondered what behavior would earn such a strong reaction.

"He was a Franciscan priest serving as Bishop of Yucatán. He took a dislike to the Mayan practice of human sacrifice—a dislike I share, of course. However, Landa did the unforgivable; he ordered his men to destroy thousands of Mayan idols and artifacts, objects of priceless value to archeologists." He clenched his fists. "Landa then compounded his crimes by burning Mayan books, all of them but four. Imagine it!" Luiz leaped to his feet and strode around his library, sweeping his hands past all the shelves. "He left only four books. And, mind you, there weren't any actual Mayans conducting pagan rituals when Landa did this in 1562; their civilization had collapsed long before."

"A terrible shame."

"It makes my blood boil to think of how he destroyed the records of my peoples' culture."

"Your people?" Anusha asked. "Are you of Mayan ancestry?"

"I am," Luiz stated with evident pride, as he returned to his seat. "In truth, it is a mixed lineage, but I consider myself mostly Mayan."

Anusha thought about how little humanity had changed since Landa's crime of erasing a culture. The violence of the ignorant knows no bounds, she mused. Despite her plea for people to continue their normal activities as time wound down to the end, many had not. With no future consequences to restrain them, people had turned violent. Crime had increased around the world, especially robbery, rape, and murder. The number of suicides, both solitary and in mass had skyrocketed. Some areas of the world had seen governmental breakdowns, with armed gangs and warlords filling the vacuum. Even those without aggressive tendencies behaved as if the end were close. The long-term economic investment markets had collapsed and a global depression had set in.

"I'm sorry, Anusha. Am I boring you?"

"Not at all. I still have a little jet lag."

"Come," Luiz stood up. "I'll take you back to the hotel."

As they traveled in Luiz's car, she saw that downtown Mexico City consisted of looted shops, broken windows, burned-out cars, and armored police vehicles on every street. The all-music radio station stopped in mid-song for a special news bulletin. More bad news, Anusha thought, in a time of bad news. "We interrupt this broadcast to bring you breaking news from India. Reports are sketchy, but it appears that a small nuclear device has been detonated within that country. The center of the blast is located in the city of Pune, some 93 kilometers east of Mumbai. You may recall that Pune was the home of Dr. Anusha Bharateeyanakshatra, known by many as Dr. Anu or the Mother Teresa of Science, the physicist who first calculated The Finality. No one has claimed responsibility for the attack, and it is not yet known if Dr. Anu was in Pune or if there are any survivors..."

In silence, tears ran down Anusha's leathery face as she cried for the loss of all the people, the people of the only home she had ever known.

***

September 22, 2012:

"Watch carefully, Anusha," said Luiz, smiling and checking his watch, "and in a few moments the effect will be at its peak."

Too frail to stand for long periods, Anusha sat in a folding chair while her bodyguards and Luiz stood beside her. They remained just outside the line that the police had marked off by ropes at the base of the pyramidal structure. The sweltering late-afternoon sun of the Yucatán did not bother Anusha; she'd spent eighty two summers in western India, so she sipped her bottled water and watched.

During the past three months, Anusha had come to appreciate Luiz both as a colleague and friend. The younger scientist had done his best to make her feel at home in Mexico City and to help her through the grief of the Pune attack.

From an oblique angle, they stared at the slanted northern face of the famous stepped pyramid at Chichen Itza. Luiz had insisted on calling it the

Temple of Kukulcan rather than its more common
Spanish name, El Castillo. With most of the temple's
face in shadow, portions of the rough, 800-year-old
stone gleamed with whiteness as the setting sun lit up
successive sections. Since they had arrived, and for the
previous several hours, it had looked like a sinuous
rattlesnake coming to life, slithering as it descended
the pyramid's angled surface. At the base of the wide
northern staircase stood the large stone heads of a pair
of serpents whose bodies formed the two staircase
railings, of which the nearest was being illuminated by
the trick of light. The famous illusion occurred at
every equinox, and only on the equinoxes.

All around them, beyond the marked perimeter,
stood a vast crowd. The throng stretched for hundreds
of yards in all directions surrounding the stone
mountain, in multi-hued contrast to the plain
whiteness of the temple. "There's always a crowd here
during the equinoxes, but never before like this," Luiz
had said. The ocean of people stood mostly silent,
except for excited murmurs here and there. Anusha
marveled at the serenity of the multitude in the midst
of such tumult around the world, and with The
Finality only three months away. Still, she knew that
even quiet groups could become provoked and excited,
forming mobs.

"I'm not comfortable in crowds," Anusha spoke
quietly to Luiz. For the first time, she felt that her
three bodyguards might be insufficient.

"We'll just stay for the final effect, and then
leave, I promise you," Luiz said.

The throng of people hushed and some pointed
at the temple. The curve of stone railing just above the
serpent heads had only then lit up. Over the soft oohs

and aahs of the throng, Anusha heard, far in the back
of the mass of people, vendors hawking snacks, T-
shirts, and other souvenirs.

"May I just speak to her, please?" a voice behind
her said in English. She turned to see Blake Denton of
CNN speaking to one of her bodyguards.

"It's all right," Anusha said to her hulking
guard. She disliked having to hire them, but the tragic
bombing of her home city had led her to wonder if the
explosion had been intended for her. Since that day,
she'd rarely appeared in public. Pune had not been the
only place to suffer. Both Tel Aviv and Damascus lay
in bombed-out ruins, Paris in ashes, Los Angeles and
Washington overrun by rioting gangs.

Denton kept his voice low after he and his
cameraman had entered the boundary of Anusha's
protection. "It's nice to see you again", he shook her
hand "I'm sorry about what happened at Pune."

"Thank you," she said.

"Say," Denton went on, "I thought the Stone
Age Mayan people didn't interest you."

Anusha thought his remark impolite, spoken
within earshot of dozens of people beside the massive
Mayan temple. Rather than answering, she introduced
Denton to Luiz.

Denton then moved on to another topic.
"We're filming the equinox phenomenon, as well as
the crowd's reactions," he said. "May I interview you
right here? I'm sure that the viewers would like to
hear your take on all this."

He had been professional to her, almost
deferential, she thought. "Perhaps—"

People around them gasped. Anusha looked
over to see that the nearest serpent head had just lit up.

The crowd broke into cheering and applause to see the full effect of the Kukulcan temple's equinoctial magic. The entire serpent became visible, undulating its way down the sloped pyramid face.

Anusha smiled at the sight, and at the evident awe of the throng. Despite everything, despite The Finality, people have not yet lost their capacity for wonder. For centuries, people had gathered here to see the strange effect. In earlier times, they had ascribed religious reasons for it. Modern scientific knowledge may have provided a more rational explanation, but the human appreciation for beauty had never waned.

A rumbling noise started at that moment, a loud grinding sound originating from the temple.

"What is that?" Anusha asked.

"I don't know," Luiz shook his head. "It has never made any sound before."

Almost everyone backed away, some with slow caution and others at a full run. A few stayed, lying prostrate before the temple in attitudes of worship. Anusha's bodyguards lifted her chair and moved her back twenty meters, where the largest portion of the crowd had retreated. The police had backed away too, though they no longer needed to restrain anybody.

"Are you getting this?" Denton asked his cameraman. They both stood not far from Anusha and Luiz.

"Yeah," said the man, trying to hold his camera and microphone steady.

"Look! It's moving!" somebody shouted.

With an immense creaking sound of stone sliding against stone, the giant pyramid was slowly moving upward. While they all watched, the thirty-meter-tall Temple of Kukulcan ascended about one meter per minute. It rose atop a new base of stone, a squat, square column of the same dimensions as the pyramid's lowest level, but with smooth, vertical faces.

Like most people on that field, Anusha gaped in astonishment mixed with horror as the stone mountain moved upward.

"It's got some kinda writing on it," said the cameraman, staring at the magnified picture on his camera. He pressed an earphone to his head. "Mr. Denton, the network wants you to go live with this in ten seconds."

Others had also seen the writing on the emerging stone surface.

"I can't read it," one said.

"Does anybody know Mayan?" another shouted.

"I will read it," Luiz said, and someone handed him a pair of binoculars.

"Look! It's stopped moving!" The ascension had ended and the Temple of Kukulcan stood about ten meters higher upon its new base.

"CNN Science Correspondent Blake Denton here. We're at the El Castillo site at Chichen Itza, Mexico where something amazing..."

Luiz adjusted the binoculars and held them up to his glasses. "It says, 'As we have sworn unto you, enter here the passage to the land beyond—no, not beyond, make that <u>after</u>—to the land after the end of seasons.' That's it; the inscription repeats, at least on the surface I can see."

"What does that mean?" a nearby tourist asked.

"The 'end of seasons' could be The Finality," Anusha said, not much above a whisper.

"Wow! It's changing again!" a voice shouted.

All around the pyramid's new base, the inscriptions started to fade and the stone slabs took on a bluish cast. The rest of the temple remained unchanged. In the span of a minute the words vanished and the base became translucent, somehow lit from within. The walls brightened, until the temple seemed to hover over a block of intense sky-blue light.

"...remarkable, unprecedented sight," Denton was saying as he faced the camera, occasionally glancing over his shoulder. "The most amazing thing I've ever witnessed. Beyond all understanding..."

"It's beautiful!" said one woman in English. She strode forward toward the temple, then broke into a run, her arms outstretched.

A handful of others did likewise. "The light! Go to the light!" one of them yelled as he ran. Some policemen tried to hold them back, but gave that up. Most people did stay back, unwilling to approach this bizarre new version of El Castillo.

The few who had rushed toward the blinding blue glow disappeared within it. Nothing marked the point where they contacted the base, if the base remained at all. No shouts of pain, no sparks of combustion; they just vanished.

"What happened to them all?" several people wanted to know.

"Luiz," Anusha tugged his arm to get his attention. "The words said 'As we have sworn unto you, enter here the passage...'" She looked at him, wanting him to confirm her thought. "Sworn unto you."

"Diego de Landa," Luiz said, slapping his forehead. "The Mayans knew all about this, knew it would happen somehow. It must have been in their most sacred writings—"

"—the ones Landa burned," Anusha said.

"...and I can now see figures actually emerging from the light..." Denton went on in a breathless, awestruck version of his broadcasting voice.

They came at a run, yelling and waving their arms. Anusha recognized the first woman who had entered, and several of the others who had rushed into the glowing base.

"It's amazing! You've got to go in and see it!" One of the men who had just come from the temple ran to Denton and the camera. He panted, trying to catch his breath. "A whole other world in there," he said in accented English. "The same air as here, same gravity. But the sun's different, and there are at least three moons. It's an entirely different planet, it must be."

"Did you meet anyone or anything in there?" Denton asked.

"No, no, I didn't. Didn't see any animals at all. But there are plants all over. Not green ones, but kind of purple..."

"Not just a different planet," Anusha said to Luiz. "It must be another universe, one that will last beyond The Finality of this one. Someone or something has built a passage from here to there. They've thrown us a lifeline."

"That someone told the Mayans," Luiz said, in a voice filled with wonder, as he gazed at the Temple of Kukulcan atop its new base of blue fire. "They knew this would occur. Even after the writings were burned, people kept gathering here at every equinox. They were all ritualized rehearsals, rehearsals for this day. My ancestors knew this would happen, and so held no fear about the end of the Long Count. It's just the beginning of a new cycle."

Anusha nodded. "See if you can get Mr. Denton's attention. The most difficult broadcast of his life is about to start."

"Huh? What do you mean?" Luiz looked at her in puzzlement.

"He must tell them all; he must convince them," Anusha said, stretching out her arm and pointing. "We have just ninety days to get seven billion people through that passage."

THE END

The Stinking One

by Chad McKee

Edward Simms had never heard such wailing. You would think the villagers were trying to wake the dead rather than put one to rest.

The procession had made slow progress in the past two hours, stopping at various alters and tiny homesteads as the ushers collected pennies for the deceased. The mourners made the contribution solemnly, placing their pennies with careful reverence on the wooden coffin. The box had been donated, as Choco had died so suddenly there was no coffin to inter his body. The man who donated it was promised a replacement post haste. He didn't seem to mind either way. There was general agreement among the villagers that it was all for naught, as the End of Days was soon upon them. There would be no one to bury their bodies because everybody would be dead in two days and with the gods of the Underworld, if the prophesy was right. Recent times had given no reason to doubt that the Apocalypse was on its way.

The sudden death of the Shaman was seen as extremely unlucky and unfortunate. Edward had to agree. Manuel Choco had been his project contact and one of the only men in the village who spoke fluent English. Edward knew Spanish, of course, but most in the village preferred *k'iche*, the native Mayan language. They now chanted and cried and screamed in their tongue, waving their arms upwards, encouraging the Shaman spirit to join with the gods of the afterlife, in heaven. The motions were more optimistic than practical, as most Mayans were fated to a dangerous journey through the Underworld, the *Xibalba*. Even Shamans.

Edward followed at the rear of the procession, allowing the villagers the freedom to bury Choco without hindrance of a *lodista*, a non-Guatemalan and a non-Mayan. Since there was no longer a Shaman priest, Choco's subordinate Diego Tantanga led the sizable cadre of *cofradia* – coffin bearers - transporting the body; Choco had been a large man. Diego hoisted a cross in accordance to the fusion of Catholicism and Mayan traditions practiced in Cat'Xotl, and murmured words from the Old Testament. Feet kicked up dust from the unpaved roads in miniature cyclones, dissipating once the wind grabbed hold. The mourners didn't seem to notice. The dusty streets reminded Edward of the drought that was slowly starving them all. The prolonged desiccation of the land had practically wiped out the corn harvest in the Highlands for the past three years, and this tiny hamlet was holding on by its stoic fatalism alone.

By the time the body was interred it was dusk, which came early this close to the onset of winter. It didn't feel like winter, not to Edward. Even in the mountains the sun baked the meadow greenery into brittle sticks of brown kindling. Recently tilled soil laid to the east. He didn't need to look over his shoulder to know that the new strains were wilting. No proper water irrigation. Even bioengineered corn needed water. He would have to talk with Diego. The young Mayan was first in charge now, with Choco passed on, and he had the village livelihood to look after.

Water was poured unto the grave and wailing men and women dropped to their knees, packing it down as Diego said his last paternoster. When the ground was made firm enough to impede any dark forces from molesting it, the procession rose once more and headed for the town center, where most would start drinking rum until the Shaman's death became temporarily irrelevant.

Edward pulled the young priest aside once in town. "Can we talk? We need to see about those crops. They're dying."

Diego nodded his head sadly. "Si, I know, Doctor Eduardo," he said. "It is a time of great sorrow."

Again with the times of sorrow. Edward had been hearing nothing but the gloom of the End of Days since he arrived in spring.

"Diego," he said patiently, "We need to have the villagers in the fields tomorrow. Otherwise everyone is going to go hungry."

"Si, Doctor Eduardo. But now the people have to think of the Shaman. He is the elder, the head of the tribe. The corn has to wait."

69

A few heads turned at the exchange. Whispers in K'iche were shared. Edward had noticed a greater frequency of dissent among the Indians. Especially now that the Shaman had passed. With Choco, Edward and the U.N. team had overcome initial resistance from the rest of the natives to plant the new corn strain. It was a traditional area, these Highlands, and wasn't open to rapid changes. Trust could only be won by first securing the edict from the center of the society – the Shaman – who encompassed the traits of politician, warrior, and mystic. The timing was bad though – the U.N. mission had touched down only eight months before the completion of the so-called Long Cycle, the end of the Mayan calendar. The End of Days. Even then there was defeatist talk concerning the harvest season – namely, why bother? Most predicted a natural disaster that would ravage most of the population. Worst of all, shamans in neighboring villages speculated that technology itself would help drive the catastrophe. People had little interest in growing what might hasten their own demise.

Some were not so certain. Bola Tiche was close by as Diego and Edward spoke. He was a farmer but one of only two people in the village who had traveled to the lowlands for work. He had been part of the sad procession though Cat'Xotl but also stayed in the last ranks, his strong, callused hands on the shoulders of his young wife. A child trailed by their feet, only three of four, eating a chili candy as he walked stolidly in sandals fashioned from strips of tire rubber.

He moved to Edward and Diego and asked in Spanish: "Doctor, do you think this village has a chance?"

"Of course I do," said Edward. "I wouldn't be here if not." He put his hand on Bola's shoulder. "I made an oath when I joined the United Nations World Food Bank and that was to provide any and every people a better chance to live. Trust me Bola, there will be no catastrophe, no End of Days. But if we don't tend the corn, we may all go hungry."

His impromptu speech was met with silence. Dire warnings had little effect when hope was already at its nadir. Instead, Bola retrieved cups and the three of them drank rum to the memory of the Shaman.

Nonetheless, at daybreak, Diego, Bola, and several villagers were out in the fields to tend to the corn. Edward gave everybody a hearty slap on the back and distributed spades and pails for water collection. He spent as much time motivating his workers as carrying out any physical work. That was the case for most of his tenure in the Highlands. Now he was the only one left of his U.N. attachment. The rest – another Briton and an American – had set about to restore crops in other Highlands valley towns. They carried a new type of corn, one developed by Monsanto in a Mexico City lab. The native corn had predictably failed for the fourth consecutive year, the vitality of the soil sapped by the never-ending heat and aridness. The village no longer had any goats and meat was reduced to chickens and a handful of pigs. The bioengineered crops were the last hope.

As the boiling day came to a close, Bola came to him. His eyes swept from side to side conspiratorially and his thick hands clasped together as if in prayer. He spoke in low tones. "So Doctor Eduardo," he began. "Can you really save us from the prophesy?"

Edward rested his hoe on the ground and used the handle as an arm rest. Before he spoke he used a sodden kerchief to clear the sweat dripping from his eyes. A Mancunian by birth, he didn't believe he would ever get used to the heat. "Of course. Like I said last night, everything will work out."

"And about the disaster?"

"What disaster?"

Bola searched Edward's eyes. "Did Choco not tell you? He revealed to me that the earth will split open tomorrow, in the middle of this corn field."

"An earthquake?" Edward stifled a laugh but his voice was heavy with doubt. "Bola, that's absurd. There's not a geological fault line for five hundred miles." He didn't actually know this but it sounded right. At any rate, he couldn't recall a severe earthquake in Guatemala in recent years.

"The earth will part," said Bola stubbornly. "And from its mouth Kisin will come carrying the wrath of the gods. Many will die unless a sacrifice is made."

"A sacrifice? What on earth are you talking about? Bola, listen to me, this is not going to happen. I respect your Shaman and his prophesies but no god is going to rise from the fields tomorrow. And if you really believed that, you wouldn't be working this field with me. Who is this Kissing - "

"Kisin. He is the god of the death, a devil, a shape-changer, he wears a collar of..."

Edward put up his hand and offered a calming smile. "Bola, I don't want to seem rude, but you must listen to what you're saying. It's not reasonable. I think that we should just..."

"I want you to take our son," he said suddenly.

72

"What?"

"Our son," Bola was saying. "Who knows who Kisin may take? You can save my son. Take him to the lowlands and back to the United Nations. Then he will perhaps avoid the catastrophe."

Edward could only shake his head in disbelief. He once more reiterated the need to irrigate the fields and to wait the short amount of time before the harvest was to be collected. Bola only repeated himself and when Edward rejected his request once more the man only stared. At some point the men in the fields began to stare as well, hoes at their sides. The dropping sun, blazing a smoky red, cast their slender forms in shadow, like a Goya painting of hell. An uncomfortable moment of tension, so common in the last weeks, passed before Edward resumed hoeing, setting an example for the others to follow. Bola refused to meet his eyes for the rest of the day.

The nights in the highlands took on a spooky cast. Despite the day's intense heat, nights were cool. Low-lying mists, the only form of moisture in the valley, occasionally settled in when the sun dropped and wouldn't clear until dusk. Edward scraped desultorily at a bowl of frijoles and a pinch of goat cheese. He sat alone in his hut, a provision given to him when he first landed in Cat'Xotl. It had not occurred to him then that the humble structure had been erected on the outskirts of the village. He was close to the corn but to little else. As each day passed what few people were in the area receded as well, leaving him with his beloved crops. The absence of people would naturally amplify all the other sounds of the night, if there were any. Edward was rewarded only with the rustling of the corn in the night wind, filtering dust through their fragile stalks.

Eventually, after writing a bit in his journal with the meal, he did start to hear something different. A low, regular, repeated sound. It was unusual enough to rouse his curiosity. After a few more mouthfuls of beans Edward convinced himself that the sound was not his imagination and that it was originating from the town center. He only hesitated for a heartbeat before putting on his windbreaker. He had to admit that his interest in the disturbance was as much a need to move from the lonely dwelling as it was curiosity.

The distance from his habitation to the town center was not long but Edward found that the closer he approached the quieter his walk. He pushed through the maze of criss-crossing alleyways formed by the tiny houses radiating outward from the village square. Most doors were open but few sounds emitted from their interiors. There was a shuffling to Edward's left, which sounded a bit like some body quietly moving in the opposite direction, reversing his path. My shadow, he thought. Within a block of the town square he was creeping, attempting to keep the crunch of rock under his boots to a minimum. It was unlike him, stealth. Honesty and openness, these were the standards of a U.N. official. These were the only ways to capturing trust. Still, he did not quicken his pace.

The town intersected at its only major roads, one of which ran towards the Salinas River, and the other in the general direction of Chiapas, Mexico. Both were paved – at least within city limits – but also dusty and unkempt, riddled with cracks and potholes. None of that mattered much on foot, the case for most of the village, which only boasted a dozen or so cars.

Nonetheless, one always heard the sounds of
domestication when walking along the roads: women
stretching work clothes over rocks, or preparing
tortillas; the men tinkering with tractors or playing
betting games; and often both genders sharing time at
the cantina, which featured local boys on battered
guitars and the town's only marimba.

Edward heard none of this as he progressed
through the Salinas Road, the moon his only
companion tonight. The sole unified sound came from
the direction of the church and it increased in volume
with each step. Edward approached the structure after
only a few minutes walk. It was the largest building in
the township, white-washed walls stretching some
fifty feet in the air if one counted the bell tower. It was
silent now but not its occupants. They were singing. It
was a hushed singing, much like a prayer, but by the
rumbling decibels of sound most of the village was on
hand. Edward's curiosity drove him to the door, where
his hand paused over the wrought iron handle. A
feeling – an intuition – caused him to hold back from
opening the solid oaken door that he had passed
through most days since he had come to the village.
Less because of his personal beliefs, but because it was
expected for everyone to give grace to Our Father for
daily gifts. Those had been few and far between,
Edward thought bitterly. But it was not his place to
interfere with the culture, only to shape its agricultural
ability.

Edward experienced a flash of hesitation when
deciding on which door to enter. There was the nave
door, of course, which would put him immediately
among the congregation. That would have been the
most obvious, but for some reason this service struck

him as unusual. Tomorrow was the end of the Tzolkin calendar, or the beginning of the end according to the beliefs of these people. It occurred to him that he might not be welcome among them as he had actively campaigned against their archaic belief system. But their singing – it was hypnotic. A repeating pattern, three words; Edward could not distinguish them through the door, but found his curiosity could not be diminished. In spite of the differences between himself and the K'iche, he had begun to feel a sort of embryonic kinship with them. He knew everything that these people did on a daily basis; his exclusion from this gathering struck him as unexpectedly alienating. It was as if he had made no inroads at all with his new neighbors.

He moved to the back entrance, using more furtiveness than he would like to admit. He turned the knob of the door that accessed the kitchen and went into the darkened room. The church may have been the largest structure in town but it was architecturally simple. The tiny kitchen was just one of three branches in a hall that acted as the church's main artery: a small rectory and a toilet were the others. At the end of the hall was the opening to the service. The chants were louder, of course, but in accompaniment was an odd squealing one couldn't here from the outside. Edward walked casually to the end of the hall, wanting to attach no significance to his concealment but feeling a knot of tension in his stomach that forbade his approaching any further than the entrance.

A partial view of the chancel witnessed numerous candles blazing, more in fact that Edward had ever seen in lit in the church. To his relief, he could see that Diego was leading the services. He was

assisted by another man, Emilio, a carpenter and
sometimes assistant at weddings and funerals. He was
also a *cofradia*. Despite the presence of the two faces,
Edward's new found comfort was short lived. This was
no mass or even a K'iche version of one. Diego was not
holding a Bible but a baby pig, its legs tied together in a
knot, hung upside down over a bowl. With a slashing
motion Diego cut the pig's throat open, letting the
blood drain into one of the bowls used sometimes for
washing linens. The bowl was a garish yellow, against
which the blood glistened brightly in contrast.

     The blood-letting did not stop there; other
bowls were circulating around the room. A thorn
accompanied each, allowing each person to tear their
skin and bleed a drop of blood. Edward's stolen glances
didn't allow him to recognize many faces but he didn't
need to – he knew the entire population – but his eyes
never left the thorn. It gouged flesh – a puncture into a
thumb, another across a vein, one more tearing into the
skin above an eye, or through a lip. Self-sacrifice - a
blood offering to position themselves favorably in the
afterlife. Old women cut themselves. So did the
children, guided by the hands of their own parents...

     Edward turned to leave but his legs didn't move;
instead, a tingling invaded his fingers and spread
quickly through his body. He took deep breaths to
combat the encroaching hyperventilation. Desperation,
he thought. That was all. The numbness spreading to
his arms was not responding to his rationalization,
however. Edward hazarded one more glance into the
sanctuary – and saw Diego staring directly at him. The
young Mayan's face was completely without emotion,
or even recognition. His dark eyes locked with
Edward's, but only for moment; he raised the bowl of

pig's blood above his head as he began that incantation again: "Kam oj kissing...oj kam la..."

Edward fled, escaping the church the way he came. Thankfully, no one followed. However, when he returned his bungalow was empty but with the feeling of recent occupation lingering. His fear returned as he considered his options – none seemed to make much sense. He had nothing to steal and it was doubtful that the thief would keep his identity secret for long – here, everybody knew what you had and didn't have. In any case, a quick search found nothing missing. Edward was nonetheless certain his home had been occupied. He shut the door and took the unprecedented action of bolting the lock. The lock itself was flimsy – it could be kicked in by most men, possibly most women – but was psychologically reassuring. He was restless with worry over the night's events. After a time of pacing along the packed dirt floor, shut in with his suspicions, he made himself lay down. It was the night of the End of Days. There was little surprise that the natives were doing some things different, going a little stir crazy. Tomorrow, when everything was normal and no catastrophe led the village to its death, order would restore itself. His analysis did little for his dreams, which featured Edward being fed to the corn and then the corn to the people.

Edward was awakened by a light knocking on the door. He tensed, the fear from the previous night reasserting itself in an instant. The light of dawn shone weakly through the curtains on his tiny window. There was a faint voice on the other side of the door. Edward remained motionless in his bed, like a prisoner summoned for the firing squad.

"Doctor Eduardo?" the voice said. "Doctor Eduardo!"

It was Bola.

"Thank God," Edward said to himself feeling foolish. He forced himself to regain self-control before going to the door.

Bola was in a state of distress. His dark face was creased with concern and stress.

"Where were you last night?" he demanded.

Edward was guarded with his answer. "Here, of course. Why?"

"You were not here," Bola said with an accusatory tone. "I came by last night and your house was empty."

So, the intruder was Bola. A person he could confide in? Edward looked for a scar on Bola, some recent ripping of flesh that would show the man had participated in last night's blasphemy in the Church. A cursory search found nothing. Still, the wound could be hidden, or small. Residual paranoia prevented Edward from disclosing what he knew. The village would be on edge all day and he would tread carefully.

"I took a walk."

"You must go today," Bola announced. "Before Kisin rises. This is for your own good."

"Bola, I told you yesterday and the day before-"

"Listen, Doctor, there is very little time. Guillermo has donated his truck for your escape. He does not believe he will need it anymore after today, so it is yours."

"Bola!"

"Doctor, please, keep you voice down! We only have moments before the others go to the field."

Edward straightened. "Yes, the field, that's exactly where they should go. And I'm going there as well."

He went to retrieve one of his work shirts, one with the UN's Food Bank logo emblazed upon the chest. He felt today, certainly, that he could remind the locals who he was and that he could help them.

"No, Doctor. Please, go to the part of the Chiapas road beyond the corn. Guillermo will meet you there and a few other villagers who appreciated the help you gave us."

"Are you still trying to give me your son?" Edward asked.

The words left his mouth coldly, more so than he intended. Bola stood quietly for a moment, as if stung, then slowly shook his head.

"No, my wife will not part with Pedro. We will face the catastrophe together, as a family."

"Sorry, you have to understand my position. I can't just leave. This village is my responsibility. And I think one of my duties is to show you that this end of days business is pure nonsense!"

Again Bola was silent. Edward cursed his lack of tact, but the importance of the day was straining his courtesy. He put his arm on Bola's shoulder and said in a friendly way:

"I'm sorry Bola. I have to stay. Why don't you retrieve your hoe? Let's show everyone that we can spit in the eye of this so-called Kisin!"

Edward rushed into the morning sun and strode directly to the fields. The temperature rose by the minute. After only half an hour he was unbuttoning the front of his shirt. Trying to ignore the heat he began inspecting the corn stalks. They were brittle.

Edward hoped that the temperature would be milder by planting so late, but that was not the case. Looking up not a single cloud shadowed the glaring sky. Planting in October! It was insane. He hoped the newest tilling would make a difference, maybe even result in a reasonable harvest if it would only rain.

Edward toiled for the better part of the early morning but none of the villagers showed as promised. He began to wonder if Bola was misinformed, or if there had been a change of plans. Supernatural fear was the root of too many problems. The understanding and application of science coupled with general education and factual information could put his village straight. But right now he felt like a lone solider fighting a war he had no hope of winning.

Eventually they did come, quietly and cautiously arriving in two and threes. They brought hoes, spades, and buckets. The turn-out was heartening once it began. Edward resumed his encouragement and marched among the rows of corn like a two star general, the hoe at his shoulder a regimental baton. He looked for Bola among the workers, a faint feeling of guilt building as the villagers worked. It would not dampen his spirits.

The work was steady until the Earth moved.

It was not a strong tremor, no larger than a stone shifting under foot. However, the effect on the villagers was immediate and most dispersed, leaving their implements behind. Edward would have been lying if he said he wasn't surprised at the tremor. For an instant his unflappable logic abandoned him, and he himself waited for the true earthquake, the destroyer of the Highlands. Tense moments passed as the K'iche left the fields in droves. Only a few stayed where they were, rigidly still, awaiting the earthen upheaval that would announce Kisin. It did not come. Edward found he had to exhale or his lungs were going to burst. If this was the fulfillment of the prophesy, everything could still be alright. Some of the villages would need more reassurance, but surely they would see reason. Edward was relieved when Diego began running after his charges.

Eventually, the residents were calmed as the priest began making soothing gestures. His hand talk seemed obvious: make a line. The villagers gradually strung themselves along the perimeter of the cornfield. Edward exchanged looks with the handful that stayed behind, but their expressions were unreadable other than fear. The thin band of people spread around the field before standing motionless in their formation. To Edward it felt uncomfortably like a net. He tried pointing to Diego, indicating for him to re-enter the field, but Diego stood silently like the rest, a spectator. The unsettling feeling Edward experienced last night returned in full force. He shouted for the villagers to return to their work but no one moved. Their lack of movement was unnerving, but the silence was far worse. The Highland people always laughed and spoke and gestured. They were demonstrative. Their protracted silence now made them strangers.

Edward's annoyance finally outstretched his patience. He put down – or rather, threw down – his hoe and re-buttoned his work shirt. If they wouldn't come to him, he would go to them. He needed water anyway. It had been foolish to not bring a canteen out to the fields. Now he would have to bring up the bucket in the well. It was an arduous process at the best of times, yet alone after the sun did its work for a few hours.

The ground moved again and this time the earth tore itself in two with a violent heave. Edward's feet came out from under him and he was propelled like a stone from a slingshot. He landed on some corn stalks several rows from where he had been standing. It was as if he completed a long jump without using his legs. The ground continued to shake after he lay on the ground – back and forth, back and forth. Dust rose up in massive cyclones making it impossible to see. Edward tried to shield his eyes and only succeeded in nearly gouging out his eye. He stopped fighting and simply allowed himself to ride the whims of the Earth as its crust folded into alarming angles.

Just as abruptly as the earthquake began, it ended. Edward did not move at first, fearing he would be tossed into the air again. With the dust so thick there was no visibility to see where you might fall. Better to wait it out. Complete silence marked the first minute or so following the quake. Then, gradually, groans of pain from the injured and cries of fear could be heard.

They were alive, though. Things could be salvaged. Edward thought back to his U.N. training. What was the appropriate response in a catastrophe? *Calm, collect, respect...* Edward shook the dust out of his hair and cleared the grime from his eyes. It was time to re-establish control.

He was just standing up as he heard the sound of footsteps. The steps were heavy, accompanied by slashing and crunching sounds. Stepping on the corn, Edward thought indignantly, until he realized there was likely no corn left. Only dust. Finally, it was beginning to settle.

A figure emerged from the haze. Edward's mind was rattled from the quake because he couldn't quite make out who the figure was – the dust appeared to shrink from the body rather than the figure move away from it. The man was imposing, that was a certainty. Muscled, legs like trees grown from the tilled soil, ribbed stomach heaving with huge breaths. Except for a thin layer of dust he stood over Edward completely naked, bronzed like a god. He did at closer glance wear a collar; a collar with oblong shapes hanging from it. They looked like something familiar... it was difficult to tell on the ground with the dust clouding his vision. It then occurred to Edward that this might be a god, this Kisin the villagers had spoken of. A moment later he was able to make out what was dangling from the man's collar: eyes, with the optic nerves still attached. Edward abruptly remembered Kisin's title. The God of Death.

Eyes so dark the irises didn't show, set in a stony face that showed no emotions whatsoever. The man's features might have been leather, or perhaps wood. The effect was of something solid, immobile. The powerful arms that hung at his side were not quite at rest; they were slightly bent at the elbow, as if ready to reach out any moment and destroy something. Edward knew then that any false move could result in his death – it was that obvious.

Still, the massive arms stayed in their resting positions, though the man's head tipped to the insignia on Edwards shirt. It seemed as if he were reading the U.N. logo on the front of his work shirt. When the eyes refastened themselves to Edward they were considering rather than hostile. He felt small, like a child under the stare of an angry father.

The answer was to reach out – communication was the key. That was the motto for all United Nations employees: diplomacy first. He put his hand in what he thought was a friendly gesture, something welcoming, even if his smile faltered on the edge of his lips. He took a step forward to encourage interaction. The hulking nude man only stared.

Making another effort, Edward spoke his name. He was shocked at how loud it sounded after the quiet that followed the quake. Despite its amplification his voice didn't seem imposing at all.

He felt his words tumble into a vacuum when the man once again did not respond. He would have tried again if a voice behind him didn't speak up. Edward recognized the words being spoken, the same ones Diego said in K'iche last night – *kam oj kissing. Oj kam la.* Not kissing, but Kisin. Of course, that would make... But he did not have long to contemplate the fact when he felt something enter his chest. Edward was dumbfounded for a second as he stared at the dagger thrust through his chest, then from the dagger to Diego. The priest wore a stony expression.

"I'm sorry, Dr. Eduardo," he said. "This is for the good of the village."

Although he didn't feel much pain, Edward fell to the ground anyway. Mostly he registered an odd heaviness in his limbs and a strong tingling sensation throughout his body. It was a replica from the previous night, only much stronger. He looked up at the sky and watched the few wisps of cloud move lazily across his field of vision. If only there could have been more clouds, he thought.

He then focused on Kisin who was presently leaning over his dying body. The bronze man grabbed hold of his arm with those powerful hands and kept hold, not uncomfortably, just firmly. His face was calm but in concentration. Edward felt light, more so with each instant. Oddly, as he looked into Kisin, he began to see his own image, as if a mirror was forming in front of his face. The effect didn't last long because his body lay dead within seconds.

He was not forgotten though. The villagers watched him as he walked purposefully, still nude, still bronzed with fine dust that glistened in the noon sun. He was led by Diego, who walked straight into Edward's room and removed a suitcase. Inside was another shirt, recently washed, with the U.N. logo, the perfect size. The shirt was donned and with it the future of the village. Now they would have a real voice.

Outside, in the baking sun, Bola looked over the body. He shook his head sadly. It could have been different. Then again, maybe this was fate. The village was not destroyed as feared. Not yet. That had been avoided and now his son might have a chance after all.

"Maybe Diego is right," he said. "Maybe our future is ours to decide."

He shared looks with the resident closest to him and softly said: "K'am oj Kisin. Oj kar la!" Accept us Kisin. We accept you!

And with that he left the crumpled body among the cornstalks, broken and scattered around the field.

Sun Born

By Wendy N. Wagner

She awoke in the gray pearlescence of pre-dawn. It was quiet, deeply, wholly quiet. She lay motionless, listening, and was finally glad for the soft sound of her own inhalations. There was no other accompaniment as she rolled her bulk off the futon.

A belly the size of hers merited a small groan, but Liz refused to spend the last weeks of her pregnancy grunting or waddling or complaining about her size. *She* was not big. The world inside her was, brimming with nourishing liquids and sheltering placenta. An entire magical habitat was cradled in her pelvis.

But her inhabitant, long used to the luxurious accommodations, was almost ready to move on. The little jabs were constant, hidden limbs digging into her organs, rearranging them. Her bladder was weary of the crush and adjustment.

She peed, ate some food, and peed again before leaving the gloomy apartment. The world still waited on dawn. The sky was gray; the shadows of trees were pale. Everything had the same wan cast of the interiors of her apartment, and for a moment she wanted desperately to go back inside, burrow under the comforter and never move again.

She lowered her gaze to the sidewalk and went on, one slow foot after another.

At this point in the pregnancy, her midwife has explained, it was best to work the body, strengthen the muscles. Labor was grueling work—more a battle between two alien bodies than a task to muscle through. A fighter needed to be strong. Liz squatted twenty minutes a day to tone her groin muscles, and walked for miles.

She walked slowly. Movement felt good, but there was no quick way to move a belly so vast. She had to be careful; her ligaments were loose with hormones, and her protruding stomach hid the ground ahead. She had to be watchful.

Her eyes scanned the ground, the street, the trees at the end of the block. Something shot over her head and then dropped, fluttering, into an elm. In silence, it watched her. She looked away from the winged shape. She reminded herself that she had seen owls in the neighborhood before. She saw lots of animals on her morning walks.

The walking began when she moved into this apartment building, after James left and she needed someplace inexpensive and close to work. She'd worried about living downtown, but it wasn't as bad as she'd expected. The area settled down at night, and she hadn't had any problem with the homeless around her building.

Her eyebrows contracted. By now she should have seen one of her street people. Pablo, with his cart full of cans, or Big-Beard with his palm out. But she was still alone, on a gray sidewalk, under a gray sky. Her lips tightened, but she put one foot in front of the other and kept on.

It took focus to keep going, an act of will, but she had become good at those things since James had left. When he first told her that he would rather follow his thesis advisor to Mexico than stay here with her and his child, it crushed her will to even breathe, let alone think or walk. She had pressed herself into the couch and begged it to swallow her like loose change.

But the tender presence inside her, at that time still barely a bulge in her waistband, reached out to her with waves of comfort. It was sensation without words, strange and wonderful, and she clung to the feeling. She clung hard enough to squeeze the rest of the world out of her vision. That was what focuses meant: a kind of blindness that hid away everything unnecessary to one luminous goal.

Even before she passed the elm tree where the owl sat, its golden gaze fixed on her rounded form, she had pushed it into the dark places she did not see. She scanned the road ahead and stepped carefully onward, toward the park.

The park was the size of a city block, with a fountain, the modern kind where squared blocks of granite seeped water until a shallow pool formed, then quietly drained away to recycle. The first time she had seen this park, her feet had been bleeding. She hadn't expected one of James's romantic walks when she picked her outfit, and the turquoise sandals were too pretty to resist. He hadn't even noticed them.

Liz settled onto one of the scattered blocks of pink stone, remembering. She had kept her feet, rubbed raw and blistered, in the trickling coolness of the fountain as James drifted into the details of Mayan creation. Like all the other Mayan stories, this one was cruel and bloody. She had to cut him off at the point where the Mother Goddess was raped by a feathered monster.

"Didn't that happen to Leda? Hercules's mom?"

He rolled his eyes. "That was a swan. Coatlicue was impregnated by ball of feathers. A ball." He leaned toward her, his blue eyes filled with an excited brightness--the same brightness she had seen when she first met him, desperate to renew four overdue books on Pre-Columbian pottery. It had charmed her. Then.

He continued. "Balls were very important to the Mayans. They played a ritualistic ball game that symbolized the gods' fights to control the sun."

Liz pulled her feet from the water, winced, and then put them back in the numbing water. "Coatlicue? She's the one with the snake skirt and the skull necklace, right? Isn't she Aztec?"

He got up. "There's overlap in the two cultures. Now come on." He put his hand out to her. "I'll buy you an ice cream."

She half-expected to hear the ice cream man's bell jingle as she came out of her memory--but of course, it was nearly the end of December, and all the ice cream carts were parked away somewhere, waiting for the first flush of sunshine to release them from their hibernation. She rubbed her palm across her belly, feeling a jolt from inside. The sensation almost made her smile.

Yesterday had been Christmas. She spent it alone, no boyfriend, no family. Her parents had promised to call from her brother's house, but he must have made the eggnog too strong again this year, because even when she tried their cell phones, no one answered. She would try again today, at a more reasonable hour. She was so eager to hear another voice. She read out loud every night to her belly, but it wasn't the same. Her own voice did nothing to pierce the silence all around her.

The white shape of an owl landed across from her. It cocked its head and made a rattle in the back of its throat.

"I don't have anything for you," she called. Her voice sounded tinny in the bowl of the fountain.

The owl shook out a wing and preened its armpit.

She recognized it. The bird had sat here yesterday, its eyes fixed on her, watching. It made her uncomfortable. The creature's beak was so large. Its talons were close to an inch long. And it was an owl. Weren't they associated with death in every culture?

Another owl landed beside the first one. It shifted from foot to foot for a few moments, then turned its predatory yellow eyes on Liz. They were both light-colored birds, with little feather tufts like horns on top of their heads.

She stood up. Keeping her eyes on the owls, she backed away a few steps, then moved as quickly as her mass would allow. She hurried down the sidewalk and

around the corner. But within a few blocks, her feet
slowed. She knew what was waiting for her ahead.

Just a few days ago, this had been her favorite
street. The shop windows were always bright and
freshly arranged, and the Italian coffee bar on the
corner pumped out waves of fresh-roasted air. It was a
cheerful and bustling avenue.

But today the air smelled only of damp cement,
and the lights were off in every window. She still
glanced at them, even though they had been dark since
the 22nd. The glass, black, stared back at her dully.

She turned her head away from them, and
crossed the street at the crosswalk. There were no
traffic signals, but she was still careful. Her pace
slowed as she walked the last few steps to the end of
the world.

Where there should be a French bistro, there
was now a wall of mist, chill and impenetrable. The
same blank gray as the sky. She could put her hands
out to it and feel it pressing back against her palms.
She'd tried, the first day. She threw herself against it,
clawing, kicking, screaming. Her efforts had only
made her clothing damp.

The mist had moved since that first day. Her
world had compressed another block and a half last
night. She felt a spasm of fear at the realization, and a
sudden clenching in her belly. She needed to walk.

But she wasn't ready to face the owls or her
apartment building. From her front door, only a row
of Victorian houses separated her from the mist's
southern boundary. But the building itself frightened
her more than that strange gray wall. She could
understand apartment after apartment standing open,
empty. She had even gone inside one unit. It took her

an hour to work up the nerve to go inside. There were no bodies, no blood. Only the hot smell of a coffee pot left on too long; a toothbrush sitting expectant, paste uncapped beside it.

These things were like artifacts not yet buried by disaster or time. Looking at them, she felt like an artifact herself, the last inhabitant of some ancient abandoned city, somehow forgotten in the end of times.

The end of times. All those pseudo-scientists, claiming December 21, 2012 was the end of the world, counting down on those crazy Mayan calendars--James had laughed at them all. But she had known, the minute she saw the wall of mist that had swallowed up her city and choked out all the sound, that James was wrong.

The mist sent out a tendril to caress the pavement before it, moving toward her. Liz's feet caught each other as she ran from that sickening gray coil. She caught herself on a mail box and forced herself to stop. She shivered, and stroked her big belly, and focused on walking, quickly, back toward the park.

The owls were still there, side by side on a pillar. They watched her walk the last few feet and settle back on her block of granite.

She stared at them; their soft feathered devil heads, and wrapped her arms around herself. "Why you?"

They made no sound. She would think them imaginary except for the white streak of dung that newly graced the rock. That spoke clearly of reality.

"There aren't even any cockroaches left under my sink. They always said that at the end of the world, cockroaches would be the last living things. Not owls."

Her mind ran over all that she knew about owls, and recollected only their nocturnal habits and some half-remembered Mayan stories. In those legends, strange owls carried messages for the lords of the underworld. They didn't shit on rocks or stalk pregnant women.

Another owl swooped over her head, dropping to the ground in front of her in the eerie silence that was normal for an owl. It stretched a foot--a red foot, as if it had dipped its leg in paint, or worse, blood--and scratched the side of its head.

The strange owl flew up to the other birds' perch, leaving behind a long, black snake.

The snake was dead.

Liz squatted beside it, looking over the slender black body with its elegant yellow racing stripe. The jaw hung aside, dislocated, giving the head a strangely flattened appearance. It was a perfectly normal dead garter snake, save for the length of it. It brought back a memory.

She had been a lonely little girl. She grew up in the country, the depths of the woods, in a tiny town connected only feebly to the outside world by the narrow trace of a two-lane road. There was no grocery store, no post office. When the road was closed, the town held its breath.

It commanded respect, that road. And with the help of both the seasonal parade of hunters and the two or three teenaged drivers in town, the road claimed its share of sacrifices. Liz, even then a walker, saw many small bodies flattened to satisfy it.

But the garter snake was special.

She saw garter snakes every day in the summer. They would lie along her driveway and bask in the sun. Some, braver, followed the drive to its mouth at the main road, and tried the heat of the blacktop. This garter snake was one such fellow, and his lot was like theirs: crushed, lifeless, tossed aside by the vicious wheels. But his body stretched long, much longer than an ordinary garter snake. He was at least as long as Liz was, and she was a lanky eight-year-old.

His grace brought tears to her eyes. She was sensitive and cried often for the creatures on the road, but these tears were impassioned. She cried for three endless minutes and then wiped the salt and snot away, and even though she was forbidden to touch anything dead, moved the snake from the highway. Its scales were like liquid made still in her fingers.

Liz, large, adult, remembered clearly what it was like to bury that snake. She remembered the incredible tenderness she felt, pouring the soil over the broken body, covering the raw black slice of earth with leaves and a mountain of dandelions. Her adult hand fumbled in her pocket for a tissue, and she plucked the snake from the ground.

There was very little green space in this park, and she had only a fragment of stick to dig with. But she managed a shallow furrow, and she settled the little body inside. It was a nice spot beneath a cherry tree.

How many graves had she dug, she wondered. After the garter snake, she made it a point to check the road every day for fresh victims. She'd recovered frogs and mice, chipmunks and possums, and once, horribly, a deer. It had taken her so long to push that one off the road, and there was no way to dig a big enough hole.

She had settled for a cairn, and that had been hard enough.

She sat back on the ground, tired. It was a small grave, but she felt drained and suddenly cold. Liz wanted to sleep until the sun came up, sleep until the panhandlers started their rounds. She felt a tear on her cheek at the futility of wishing, and she brushed it away with fingers sweet with the smell of turned soil.

The owls shifted on their stone. Liz looked up at them, unsurprised that they were still watching her. Liz folded her arms over her belly and watched them back. There was something unearthly about their hunched shoulders and wide yellow eyes, something spoke of the night and that darkness which lay beyond nighttime, the kind of darkness dealt by cruel talons and fierce hooked beaks.

They were creatures of death.

The owls made one of their strange rattling sounds, and Liz's belly, mounded warm in her arms, clenched itself, and then went still.

A complete stillness, without motion or the wonderful comforting presence she had grown used to sensing inside her. There was another burning flash of cramping.

The pain of it made her whimper, and the sound drew one of the owls to her. It sat just out of reach, its strange wide-eyed face unreadable. Unreadable as the smooth expanse of her abdomen, but just as ominous.

She breathed as the clenching in her belly relaxed, and she reminded herself that it was normal for babies to settle into sleepy readiness at the end of their term. Normal for the uterus to flex its muscles in those irritating practice contractions. Her midwife would have told her all the same things. Would have, of course, if she still existed somewhere in the middle of all that gray fog.

A sob caught in her throat, and the owl hooted. Liz swiped at her tears with her arm and looked up at the creature. Its nictitating membrane passed across its pupil, a saurian eye blink.

She had to look away. The sky was still gray. That hadn't changed, not since she'd gotten up on the morning of the 22nd sometime before dawn. The sun just hung, somewhere beyond the gray curtain, not willing to come up and not ready to disappear.

Something landed beside the owl then.

It was an owl's head, oversized, with wings. It settled onto the grass and stared at Liz. Without a body, its beak was somehow more malevolent, like a dully gleaming obsidian knife.

It hopped toward her with a sound like a grunt.

She crawled away, backward, and it stopped.

She froze.

The owl with the red foot flew off the stone pillar and swooped down beside the owl-head. It struck at the ground with its strange limb and loosened the earth she had so carefully mounded over the dead garter snake.

"No! Stop that!"

It turned its head over its shoulder and chattered at her. She pounded the ground and growled at it.

It scratched at the ground again, its scarlet leg like blood or flame against the raw soil. The grave was shallow, and already the snake's tail showed. The owl pinched it in its beak. She wanted to strike it, take the snake away, but the other thing was in her way, a bouncing ball of feathers.

The red-footed owl pulled the last inches of the snake from the ground and shook the dust from it. The corpse's skin, sleek and glossy even in death, caught the sun's weak light and gleamed.

A contraction squeezed Liz's body. She collapsed on her side, gasping.

The owls hooted to each other. Over the wracking cramps, she felt something thud down on her hip, gripping sternly. She screamed at it, but it didn't move.

The owl laid the snake's body on her thigh, and she watched the snake curve over her legs, lengthening into loops, winding up and down into the drapery of a skirt, a serpentine skirt, and she struggled to sit up and pull it away. The owl pecked at her fingers, and another cramp drove away the world.

The owl-head hopped onto her belly. It burned with heat.

"Get off me!" Her voice was savage.

The owl-head pulled its wings to itself and pushed against her thighs. Her thighs stung and smoked. She clawed at the thing, but it slid away from her fingers, slippery, hot, and somehow slick. Her underwear flaked into ash and her core burned.

She screamed pain and rage.

Her waters poured out of her, a great birthing flood, and she saw the owl-head pushed aside by the torrent and her hands moved into claws, catching and gripping its wings in her fists. Blood, red coursing lava, streamed from its body and burst the grass around her into flames.

She screamed again, but this time the bellow of contraction. She pulled herself to squatting. A tiny part of her wondered how her feet could be bare, and how her thighs could be so wide and strong, but that part was slipping away, quieted by a fierceness within her. Her toes gripped soil gone muddy in the liquids of her labor, and she pushed.

Pushing, light broke across her retinas, and she couldn't be sure if it was the pressure in the delicate blood vessels or true light, like sunbeams in her face. But as she waited for the next contraction, breathing for it, she could see that the park was gone, the fountain, the surrounding buildings. There was only gray blankness and the mud beneath her, and the owls, their faces tipped up at her. The owl-head gripped in her hands bounced to the rhythm of her breath, and the serpentine skirt wriggled. Its scales were warm now, and she wasn't surprised to look down at her knee and see the black head complete, its tongue darting between its lips, its lidless eyes bright.

She ripped her dress open to let the warmth of her skin out into the mist. The next contraction came and this time she saw the light beaming from her scarlet vulva, and the sun crept up on the horizon, and she laughed and she pushed and she felt hot tears on her cheek. Tender wings brushed them away.

Her baby tumbled onto the back of the red-footed owl. His skin gleamed and gave up streamers of pale, fine smoke, and he laughed with the sound of birdsong in the morning.

But she was not done yet.

She pushed again, her cry huge, turning to a wind that parted the last tendrils of gray mist. The second baby crowned, dark hair soft and damp. She stretched her hands to catch her son, and she knew her fingers were still black with the soil of the snake's grave. For this child, she knew that was right. Her son's shoulders settled into her palms, and the placenta followed. Its velvet folds unfurled into fields of grass and wildflowers. The wind of her birthing cry circled the new earth and returned to stroke the luxurious growth.

The Mother dropped down in the soft grass, her cheeks streaked red with her womb's blood and black with earth. She brought her twins to her great bosom, smiling. They drank the thin colostrum, and their skins glowed with the vigor of it.

The owl-head bobbed once to her, and once again to his dark son, then flapped its wings, flying for the forest that stretched where once a city had been swallowed up in mist. The red-footed owl brushed its beak against her finger, joining the others, speeding for the trees.

The sun had come up. And owls were nocturnal creatures.

Revealing

By Jennifer Greylyn

The music threads through her fitful dreams, gently but insistently pulling her out of them. A solitary drum, distant but sounding like a second heartbeat, throbs below her ribs. It quickens her own heart with long-held desire and makes sleep impossible...

***

The site had barely opened but it was already packed. I tucked my ticket into the pocket of my khaki shorts and made myself concentrate on what our guide was saying as the last of our tour group passed through the entrance and reassembled a short distance away.

"Chichén Itzá means 'at the mouth of the well of the Itza'," he was explaining in excellent English with astonishing composure. Astonishing because he was a short, elderly man, with a stocky build who was dwarfed by the taller, much younger and much more expensively-dressed people gathering around him. It must have been intimidating but he showed no signs of being uncomfortable. I would have been and I was used to addressing crowds but not when they were pressed so close.

If anything, however, our guide seemed to thrive on our attention. His deep and resonant voice, tinged with something more exotic than Spanish, easily triumphed over the voices of the other guides and their groups, the vendors selling the usual souvenirs and the random tourists overwhelmed by the huge stone structures that had been reclaimed from the rapacious jungle greenery.

"The Itza were an ethnic group among the ancient Maya," he continued, his white head constantly swiveling to look up into the faces, pale and dark and every shade in between, of our very diverse group. "Their name is usually translated as 'Magicians of Water'."

"What water?" a man, American by his accent, wanted to know, grinning like it was a joke. I could understand that. The only visible water was in the plastic bottles many of us carried against dehydration. It was spring—April 6, to be exact—and not yet mid-morning, but the day was already fiercely humid.

"Is it that well you mentioned?" asked a Chinese woman, more reserved and more perceptive. I liked the sound of it and imagined jumping in to cool off. Between the ever-shifting crowds and the unaccustomed mugginess, my skin was crawling with sweat. It was like standing in a warm ocean so dense with fish they kept swimming into me.

Our guide tapped his prominent nose, chuckling. "Wait and see. Just wait and see. Now if you'll follow me..." He, very cagily, trailed off and began to walk away. Our group automatically parted for him and fell in behind him.

I would have too except he paused beside me. "Would you be so kind as to lend me your arm?" He must have noticed my pained expression and was trying to distract me because he seemed too spry to need my help. Besides, he already had a cane. But it would have been rude to refuse. I stuck out my elbow.

He put his knobbly, brown hand on it and resumed walking, taking us toward the rosy-beige pyramid dominating the middle of the vast site. I found I could breathe a little easier because everyone else gave us some space.

In a much lower tone, he said to me, "All the Mayan sites are very busy these days, what with the so-called Mayan Apocalypse coming up later this year. Be thankful you weren't here a few weeks ago. Then, even more people than usual flooded in to see the shadow of Kukulkan on his temple."

A smile, sharp and mocking, distorted what had before been a broad and craggy, if genial, face. It took me by surprise, but I also smiled, because I'd read in my guidebook about how, during the spring and fall equinoxes, a shadow was cast on the north side of the pyramid that supposedly resembled a plumed serpent. Just the notion of a snake with feathers was funny, but I'd got the impression foolish people believed watching it slither along the stairs as the sun moved would bring them good luck.

Then I thought about Kate and any amusement I felt evaporated. The reason she and I were here was even more far-fetched.

***

Kate wasn't with me on the tour of Chichén Itzá, but we had come to Mexico together. It wasn't a vacation though. I'd come to support her while she had what I thought would be the latest in a series of procedures from the Cenote Clinic, a pioneer in the field of fertility. I didn't discover the truth until after we arrived and had been shown to our room.

"You're either pregnant or you're not, sweetheart," I said to her, fighting to keep my voice calm and reasonable, but anger was simmering just below the surface. "You can't be 'partly' pregnant."

"I'm explaining this badly," Kate sighed, getting up from the bed where we were both sitting and pacing restlessly. At forty-five, just a couple of years older than me, she was still slim and graceful, her short blonde hair floating like mist around her face. The glints of silver in it, like the lines around her eyes and mouth, only added a richness of character as far as I was concerned.

But she didn't see her small signs of age that way. To her, they were mounting evidence of a terrible conclusion: she would never have a child of her own. She'd been trying for ten years, six longer than I'd known her. It had become an obsession. She'd freely admit that. What she couldn't see, however, was how vulnerable it made her.

"The director, Dr. De Luna, explained it so clearly!" Kate exclaimed. She stopped and fixed her violet eyes on me, luminous with excitement. She looked very beautiful in that moment, but my heart sank. Whatever was going on, it had got her hopes up and I just knew it wouldn't be long before they came crashing down.

"Sweetheart, I think you should—" I tried to speak, holding out a hand to her, but she cut me off, acting like she didn't even hear me. Closing her eyes, she murmured, "Dr. De Luna said I'm like a field that has been sown. The seeds have been planted. Now all I need is a little rain. Something to help them grow."

I couldn't suppress a furious groan. It was worse than I'd feared. Maybe I should have realized we were going to be made fools of when our flight was booked for April 1. But I didn't believe in omens or any of that mystical mumbo-jumbo. All I knew was, less than a week ago, the Cenote Clinic had told Kate that she had to go to Mexico right away. More specifically, she had to go to their home office, which was located on an old hacienda called the Villa Ixchel just outside Mérida, the largest city on the Yucatán Peninsula in south eastern Mexico.

I'd been suspicious of the short notice. It seemed designed not to give Kate the time to think the matter through. It was like they were testing how desperate she was. I'd also been suspicious of the location. Why couldn't the new procedure be done at the branch of the clinic in Toronto, where we lived, like all the previous ones? That made me think it was of questionable legality. Maybe it was even something that could threaten her overall health. But, when I'd laid out my concerns, she'd brushed them aside.

Just like she did now. "Don't be like that," she appealed to me, her lovely eyes open again and very earnest. "Dr. De Luna promised me this new treatment would work. She said I've proven my suitability by coming here. We just have to have faith."

I was even more dubious now and couldn't keep the sarcasm out of my voice. "Did you get that in writing?"

She glared at me. "You know the clinic is reputable. You checked it out for yourself."

It was true. I'd done meticulous research into the Cenote Clinic before I'd let her sign on with them a year ago, when they'd opened their Canadian branch. I couldn't stop her from being disappointed, but I could keep her from being cheated. The clinic was secretive about their methods but well-respected in their field. More importantly, they'd never had any lawsuits filed against them. That, in itself, was remarkable.

And I couldn't complain about how they'd treated Kate. In Toronto, they'd been professional and even compassionate when nothing seemed to work. Here, everything was clearly designed for the comfort of their clients and their clients' partners. We were staying in a grand adobe house that had been renovated into a modern, luxury hotel and we'd been offered tours of the medical facilities on the estate as well as excursions to places of local interest.

No expense was being spared to make us feel welcome, but, then, it wouldn't be, would it? The fees Kate and the other clients paid were exorbitant. At best, this sounded like a scheme to squeeze more money out of people who'd do anything to get pregnant by dropping them in an unfamiliar location and playing on their desperation. I let out another groan, which emerged more as a growl.

"There are no guarantees in this business, sweetheart," I told her, my tone colder than I meant it to be as I struggled to control my temper. "You know that better than anyone."

Her eyes widened. "I can't believe you just said that." She whirled around and ran into the bathroom, locking the door.

I stared after her, stunned, my anger draining away. Then I threw myself off the bed, knelt down by the door, pressed my cheek to it. I could hear her crying. "I'm sorry. I'm sorry," I said over and over for what seemed like forever until she came out. Wordlessly, I took her in my arms and we went back to the bed.

We lay down and I stroked her flyaway hair. "Tell me about this new treatment," I encouraged her, trying to be open-minded, but she just shook her head and turned away from me, staying silent. I lapsed into silence too, but my anger returned, blazing so hot I was almost shaking.

***

...More drums join the first, calling her just to the edge of consciousness. Then a new sound overtakes them, higher-pitched, like a horn but no horn she has ever heard. It keens through her, a summons she cannot ignore. Knowing it is what she has been waiting for without knowing what it is, she rises...

***

After the Temple of Kukulkan, we spent the rest of the morning exploring the northern portion of Chichén Itzá. I could tell from the wide eyes and rounded mouths of my companions, even if I couldn't understand most of the languages they were speaking amongst themselves, that they were awed by the grand structures silhouetted against the emerald jungle.

I supposed I should have been too. The Great Ball court, for instance, easily rivaled a modern stadium or arena in size but was made without the benefit of our modern technology. The ancient Maya didn't even have iron tools. But I was having trouble taking much in. I'd got past my initial discomfort over the crowds and the heat. Now I was worrying about Kate.

Our guide, still attached to my arm, kept trying to engage my interest but didn't have much luck. Once, I raised my head when we were moving among the forest of squared columns that half-surrounded another pyramid, the Temple of the Warriors, because he mentioned the name of our hacienda.

The Villa Ixchel, I learned, was named for a Mayan goddess of medicine and childbirth. Our guide pointed his wooden cane toward a strong-featured older woman wearing a spiraled snake as her headdress who strode fearlessly among the many men, armed with spears and clubs, cut into one column.

I could understand why a fertility clinic would call its home office after her. She looked like a formidable figure. Inevitably, that led my thoughts back to Kate. She'd insisted on staying behind and she could very formidable too, especially when she set her mind on something. I sighed gloomily and pretended not to see our guide's frown of concern.

Apparently I'd been quiet for so long that it came as a great surprise to him and the rest of the group when I finally spoke. It was nearing noon when I heard him say a particular word and, without thinking, burst out, "Cenote? Does this have something to do with the clinic?"

Every pair of eyes, most sensibly shaded by some kind of hat against the intensifying glare of the sun, swung in my direction. I felt a flush start up my

neck but refused to look away. An indulgent chuckle
from our guide dissolved the tension.

"In a way, in a way," he answered, clearly not
offended and relishing the chance to be cryptic. Then,
with a deliberate wink at me, he began again. "As I was
saying, we're coming up to something known as the
Cenote Sagrado. Remember I talked about a well? This
is it. The Sacred Well."

Like most of the other parts of the site, there
was a rope barrier around the cenote to prevent tourists
from getting too close and even a few uniformed
officials on patrol to enforce it. There were irritated
mutters from many in our group about this, but it
seemed a wise precaution to me. I immediately saw
that my prior notion of jumping in to get cooled off
could have disastrous results.

The water in the cenote, shimmering like green
obsidian, looked to be some thirty meters below us.
Above it were circular walls of grey-white stone,
overhung with lush branches and vines. Cool air
drifted up from the shaft and some in our group
ventured closer to breathe it in when other tourists had
seen enough and moved out of the way. But I hung
back, wary.

"Why is it sacred?" asked a woman who
sounded German.

Another woman, an Australian, laughed, good-
humouredly but with a hint of asperity. "You've
obviously never lived somewhere that's prone to
drought. Any water's sacred then."

Our guide was nodding. "That's quite true.
Fresh water has always been a problem in Yucatán. It's
made worse by the fact we have no above-ground
rivers. The ancient Maya valued cenotes like this one

because they provided access to the water below the surface."

"So the well's natural?" queried a man who might been from South Africa. I wasn't sure about his accent.

"A natural formation, yes," agreed our guide, moving toward it and tugging me along with him. "It's a natural sinkhole that formed when the limestone in the ground caved in. But you can see the walls have been reinforced."

Only some of our companions looked. The others seemed bored, glancing around them as if they wanted to move on. I couldn't blame them. This part of the site lacked the elaborate carving we'd seen elsewhere, like the warriors marching into battle and a goddess giving them comfort. Maybe the images that reflected how the ancient Maya had seen the cenote just hadn't survived.

"Of course there was another reason the ancient Maya believed this cenote and others to be sacred," offered our guide, almost as an after-thought, casually rubbing his whisker less lip. But he didn't deceive me. His night-black eyes were very intent.

Everyone turned toward him. He made us wait for a moment and then delivered his words like a revelation. "It was a portal to the Otherworld. The realm of the gods. That's why it's also known as the Well of Sacrifice. Desperate for what they needed, the ancient Maya were willing to pay any price."

I drew in a startled breath, almost glad Kate hadn't come. She would find the idea all too familiar and probably even agree with it.

***

No matter how much I prodded, Kate wouldn't give me any details about the new procedure she was expecting to undergo. She must have known something because she had several more meetings with the clinic's director. She claimed they weren't talking about the treatment so much as her attitude toward it, but I didn't believe her.

"Dr. De Luna says my mental state is more important than my physical health," Kate told me on our third day in Mexico, April 3, when we were riding an air-conditioned tour bus into Mérida to do some shopping and see the historic colonial heart of the city.

"I need to think about why I might not have been ready to have a child before now. Why the universe might have kept me waiting." She sighed, a sad sound that pulled at my heart, and I felt a swell of anger, the same anger that had been bubbling in me since we'd arrived. "It has nothing to do with the universe, sweetheart. It just hasn't worked out so far."

Kate nodded but there was no agreement in it. She spent the rest of the trip staring out the tinted window, a frown of concentration between her pale brows. Although she was still beside me, I felt like she'd somehow passed through the dark glass. I could see her but not reach her.

On the fifth day, as we were sitting in a dim bar in Cancún and enjoying cool drinks after a stroll through the sun-baked streets, Kate informed me, "Dr. De Luna says there is a purpose behind everything. There was a reason I couldn't have a child before now. The universe wanted me to wait."

Her voice had regained its usual brightness, but I sensed it was a little forced. I leaned forward in my chair, searching her face and not liking what I saw.

The dark shadows under her eyes suggested that she wasn't sleeping very well. The uneven redness of her lips where she'd been chewing at them in worry.

I was getting very sick of hearing Kate parrot the director's words like they were holy wisdom. I didn't even think they were worth listening to. But I'd learned my lesson in letting my temper get the better of me. So I chose my words with care. "Sweetheart, you don't have to go through with this procedure. Whatever it is. We could go home right now."

Her chair scraped the tiled floor as she suddenly pushed it back and stood up. "I need some time to myself. Some time to think. I'll meet you back at the bus." And she walked out before I could say anything, gone in a flash of sunlight that died when the door swung shut behind her.

I settled the bill as quickly as I could and raced after her, but I couldn't find her. The streets were too thick with people. All I could do was make my way back to the bus and hope she showed up. She did but remained distant for the whole trip back to the Villa Ixchel. By then, I was too upset to talk anyway. I decided it was time I went to see the director for myself.

I waited until Kate had laid down for siesta in the late afternoon and then made my way to the director's office. She wasn't there but her assistant was, looking like he could use a nap himself. I insisted he call Dr. De Luna and let me into her office while I waited. I prowled around, agitated and impatient, noting the neat mahogany desk and long leather couch, then glancing at the eclectic things hanging on the walls.

Three medical degrees in various fields that
looked legitimate. A detailed map showing the
locations of the Cenote Clinic's many branches around
the world. A very large painting, the size of a mural,
that was a frenzy of bold colors enclosed at the top and
the bottom by the serenity of starry darkness. In spite
of myself, I was drawn toward it and so absorbed by it
that I didn't hear the director come in.

Flustered, I whipped around as she, not much
older than I but supremely more elegant and poised,
greeted me by name and said she was glad to have the
chance to speak with me. It was hardly the reception
I'd expected, even though we'd met before in Toronto.
It was her practice to travel around to all the clinics
and personally oversee them. She'd defused my
suspicion then, so maybe I shouldn't have been
surprised she'd be ready for my anger now.

Acting like we were only here for a friendly
chat, Dr. De Luna inclined her head toward the
painting, the silvery coil of her pinned-up hair bobbing
slightly. "What do you think of it?"

Caught off-guard, I could only say, "I don't
understand it." But she favored me with a warm smile
like that was the right answer. "Many things seem
confusing or strange when we first encounter them.
Look again."

I did, not because she told me to but because
there was something very compelling about the
painting. This time, I sensed a progression to it. On the
far left, there were animals, gold-eyed jaguars and
orange parrots and grey rabbits. Then there were
people of mud, slick brown and beige and black. Then,
there were people of wood, looking like they'd been

hewn from a primordial forest. Lastly, there were humans in a field of sun-bright corn.

"It's by a local artist," explained Dr. De Luna, coming up to my shoulder. I should have been uncomfortable at her closeness, but I wasn't. "An interpretation of the creation myths of the ancient Maya. I keep it here because so many people are fearful of what's been called the Mayan Apocalypse. They think it means the end of the world."

"You mean it doesn't?" I asked, raising my eyebrows as if I was someone who believed the panicky news reports that every new natural disaster was a sign of imminent global collapse. I had the feeling that this was more than a casual talk to divert my attention. She wanted me to hear this. I chose to play along but not too nicely.

Her smile thinned at my disingenuous tone, but her voice remained smooth and pleasant. "Thanks to the Spanish conquistadors, much of what the ancient Maya believed has been lost. But enough of their writings survive to suggest they expected it wouldn't be the end. Rather, they anticipated the beginning of a new era. It had happened before."

That was reflected in the painting. Each scene, from left to right, was blurred along the edges. The first faded to become the second, the second the third and the third the fourth. But I was reminded of something I'd been reading and I didn't think the transition was always as peaceful as the painting suggested. "Didn't some of the previous eras end in death and destruction?"

"One did," she admitted, after a brief hesitation. "The people of mud were washed away by a flood." She gestured toward the second scene with a well-manicured hand. "But it was the exception. The animals that were created first lived on. So did the people of wood who came later, although they were transformed into monkeys."

Dr. De Luna stepped away from me to approach the painting and I was startled by the pang of loss I felt. It made no sense. "We can see in their fates a lesson for ourselves. We can't ignore the will of the gods." She was gazing at the painted figures with a bizarre mix of empathy and reproach, then indicated the stretches of starry darkness framing them. "This represents the Otherworld. The realm of the gods. Below during the day. Above during the night. Look close and you can see the faces of the gods."

I moved up beside her but only to get a better look at the stars. They did seem to form faces, several looming above and below each scene. One, long-nosed and fang-mouthed, hovered over the fourth scene and looked particularly menacing. "Who's that?"

"Chaac the rain god. He was of special importance to the ancient Maya." She traced his face with a long bronze finger, almost lovingly, and part of me hoped she'd do the same to my face when she turned to me. But she only said, "We seldom speak of gods these days. Instead, we tend to say the universe. But, whatever terms we use, the truth doesn't change. What we do has an effect on the world we live in. We need to remember that. To listen to it."

Then, unexpectedly, she touched my shoulder and a wave of soothing calm flowed through me. The anger I'd barely been able to contain for days went away like it had never been. I took one, free breath and then almost choked when my brain kicked in. I was a lawyer. I was used to people trying to manipulate each other. I didn't know how the director was doing it, but she was clearly manipulating me.

I clung to that certainty as she stared into my face, radiating trustworthiness and sincerity. "Change can be frightening, I know. But you don't have to fear it." I had the sense we weren't talking about the Mayan Apocalypse anymore but something much more personal. "The truly worthy will always rise to the occasion. You could be one of them."

Her voice had fallen very low, but somehow it echoed through me. I was almost trembling. It felt like she was staring into my soul. I wondered what Kate had been telling her about us. About me.

A feeling of violation surged through me, obliterating the calm, reviving the anger. It left me dry-mouthed but reminded me of why I'd come to confront Dr. De Luna. "I want to know why you've brought us here. What's going to happen to Kate?"

She broke off her gaze with what might have been a flash of disappointment. It was hard to tell because, when she looked back, she was perfectly composed. "All in good time. Be patient. Don't judge us before you see the results."

As answers went, it was frustratingly vague and not at all reassuring. I wanted to demand more from her, but I didn't trust myself. She had some kind of power over me. I told myself it was because I was on her turf. She hadn't affected me this way in Toronto. But then I'd had Kate beside me. We'd been together. Solid and supporting each other, the way a couple should.

I'd come to see the director for Kate's sake, but I knew Kate wouldn't see it that way. She'd feel like I was going behind her back. If she found out, which she probably would. Even if Dr. De Luna didn't tell her, she had only to wake up from siesta and find me gone. Then she'd guess.

Panicked, I ran from the office without another word, somehow knowing it was already too late. Dr. De Luna simply watched me go with inscrutable eyes, showing no surprise and making no effort to stop me.

***

...More horns blend with the first. The music is complete. It awaits only her and those like her. She has no hesitation in following it. It represents everything she has dreamed of. She and the other women leave their rooms, emerging into the star-shot night. They abandon the modern buildings and slip into the timeless wilderness beyond....

***

"Water. That's what they needed most," someone ventured as our group stood around the cenote, the Sacred Well, the Well of Sacrifice at Chichén Itzá. I didn't see who spoke. I was too focused on our guide, wondering what he was going to say next.

At my side, he rewarded the remark with a wrinkled smile. "Yes, that was part of it. The ancient Maya needed water just like the rest of us" He glanced at a few of the water bottles we were carrying and drew some small smiles in return. Most of us, however, were too rapt to appreciate the humor. We just wanted him to keep talking.

"But remember I said the Itza were associated with water magic." It wasn't exactly a question, but I nodded along with everyone else, all anxious to prove we'd been paying attention. "This cenote meant more than just water to them and the other ancient Maya. It was also a place of pilgrimage. People would travel here from all over to speak to their gods. To communicate with the Otherworld. That was even more important to them."

Many of our companions were gazing at the deep green pool with new interest, but just as many were watching our guide, perhaps struck as I was by how much he resembled the carven figures on the walls, lintels and columns that we'd passed earlier. I no longer felt the lack of them here. We had him. He could have been one of the ancient Maya who'd built this place.

It wasn't really that strange. I'd read that the Maya were still very much alive and I'd seen quite a few locals this week with their short stature, thick hair and dark eyes. However, there was something different about our guide, an affinity that went beyond appearance. He was also different from the other guides we'd had on our other tours, like this was more than a job to him. I suspected the difference lay in his passion for his people's history and culture. Sharing it with tourists like us must have been what kept him working at an age when he should have been in a retirement home.

Not that he looked frail or old at this moment, though. He spoke with such energy, he seemed a towering, almost youthful figure. "The ancient Maya wanted very much to speak to their gods. When they came here, they wanted to speak to one in particular. The rain god, Chaac. They'd ask him to send the rain their crops needed to grow and thrive. But they hoped for more than that. They hoped he might also tell them what the future would be."

The future. That word resounded in my skull and drowned out everything else for a moment. It threw me back into the fog of despair I'd been in all morning, making me think of Kate and wondering if we had a future. She hadn't spoken to me since I'd burst back into our room and she'd demanded to know where I'd been. I was too shaken to lie to her. As I'd feared, she felt betrayed when she found out I'd spoken to the director. She gave up even the pretence of us spending time together and refused to come with me today.

My eyes roved over the two dozen or so other people in our group. All happy couples, many hand in hand. And who was I with? Our guide. I suddenly couldn't stand the sight of them or him. Fighting tears, I stared down at the hard ground, pale limestone, and then at the cenote itself, rippling green. Had it appeared all of a sudden on some long-ago day? Was someone standing over it when the ground collapsed? Did they feel the way I did right now? Like something you took for granted, never imagined would crumble, had fallen away under your feet?

"Take it easy, young lady," our guide murmured when my knees buckled.

I tried to shake him off with a gruff response. "I'm fine."

But he wouldn't let go, pinning me with a pointed look. Once again, I got a glimpse of something shrewd and knowing beneath his amiable exterior. Raising his voice, he reminded everyone of the dangers of getting dehydrated and suggested we all have something to drink, giving the impression that was the cause of my momentary weakness. Water bottles were dutifully unscrewed and passed around. I drank from mine and felt a little better for it. Once our guide saw I had, he resumed where I'd interrupted him.

"The ancient Maya believed sacrifice was necessary to speak to the gods. Chaac was no exception. Professional divers have dredged the sediment at the bottom of the cenote and found all kinds of artifacts. Gold, jade, pottery, incense. All expensive things. All things valued by the ancient Maya. But they weren't enough for Chaac."

Our guide paused. I might have thought it was for dramatic effect except that he was visibly searching for the right words. When he continued, there was an earnest note in his voice. "You need to understand. Chaac gave the ancient Maya rain and prophecy. Two things they believed were essential to their lives. That, in turn, merited a sacrifice that was more precious than treasure. That's why divers have also found human remains. The bones of men and women. Even children."

There was a gasp from most of the people in our group. The women automatically touched their bellies. I didn't. It wasn't that the thought of human sacrifice, especially children, didn't horrify me. It did. But I'd never imagined myself as a mother. I'd grown used to the idea of being a parent to any baby Kate might have, but I'd never wanted one of my own.

Maybe that was at the heart of our problem. The director even hinted at it. I'd never offered to get pregnant and Kate resented me for it. But it wasn't like we'd ever talked about it. And why should I have even considered it? It was Kate whose face grew soft whenever we passed a baby in a stroller. Kate who had to stop, kneel down and peer into its tiny face. Kate who had to spend long minutes talking to its mother or father while I hung back, arms folded, looking forward to moving on.

"Historians and archaeologists don't know how the ancient Maya chose who would be sacrificed to Chaac, but a story survives that suggests people didn't usually volunteer." Our guide fixed his very black eyes on the cenote, like he was seeing something that had happened long ago. "Once there was a man named Hunac Ceel. He lived in another city, Mayapan. He came here as a pilgrim and saw a number of unwilling sacrifices being given to Chaac.

"It seems like Chaac was satisfied with unwilling sacrifices when he kept sending the rain. At least the story doesn't mention anything about a drought. But Chaac needed something more in order to give the ancient Maya knowledge of the future. Hunac Ceel figured this out. He watched as all the people who went into the cenote died. If they came back at all, they were drowned and in no shape to deliver a message from Chaac.

"So Hunac Ceel decided to do something very brave. He offered himself as a sacrifice. He dove into the cenote and was gone so long everyone was afraid he was dead too. But, just as they were giving up hope, he resurfaced. He was pulled out and he told them he had a prophecy from Chaac. Chaac said that Hunac Ceel would become the new ruler of Mayapan. And it came true. He went back to his home and eventually became its new king."

The man sounded like an opportunist to me, someone who'd said what would benefit him, but I didn't voice that opinion aloud. For someone who'd mocked the shadow of Kukulkan, our guide showed genuine belief in this story and there were receptive expressions on most of my companions' faces. One of them clearly took the story a little too seriously, though, because he asked, "Do people still jump into the pool?"

His wife nudged him in the ribs and he threw everyone a sheepish look, but our guide offered a solemn reply. "Some have tried. That why those gentlemen are here." He aimed a respectful nod at the nearest uniformed official and the official nodded back, running a wary gaze over our group. A few of my companions shifted nervously. "It's happened a lot more in recent months. No one's succeeded. But those who try say they want to know what the Mayan Apocalypse will bring."

There was silence or as much silence as was possible in such a crowded place. I became aware again of the noise from the rest of the site, especially other groups and unaccompanied tourists who were eager to get close to the cenote. Our guide must have realized this as well because he raised his cane to get our attention and moved us off.

A short distance away, where the bare limestone became well-trampled grass again, he planted that cane with an audible thud and we all stopped instantly. We were accustomed to obeying him by now. For the first time, I noticed how intricately carved his cane was, the mahogany beautifully shaped into a series of zigzags. I didn't understand their significance and forgot about it when he spoke.

"I want all of you to know something about the Mayan Apocalypse." His voice had become very authoritative. It was like telling us about the cenote, Chaac and Hunac Ceel had changed something for him. He ceased to be the charming old man everyone expected and let us all see the depths of intelligence and confidence only I'd previously glimpsed.

"It's very misleading to call it an apocalypse, considering what 'apocalypse' usually means in English. Something destructive. Maybe the end of the world. That's misleading too, by the way. Its original meaning was quite different. It meant something that was uncovered or revealed."

He swept his now-fierce eyes over all of us, in particular squinting up at me. I fought not to flinch. "Remember that because it's more like what the ancient Maya would have believed. They had a lot of different ways of reckoning time. One you folks may find interesting is the *tzolkin*, a 260-day calendar based on the average length of a human pregnancy."

A good-humored smile briefly eased our guide's sternness but didn't last long. "The prediction of the Mayan Apocalypse is based on another calendar known as the Long Count. It runs into the millennia. The ancient Maya believed there had been previous races of people. Each one was flawed in some way and didn't please the gods. Humans have lasted a long time, but the ancient Maya thought change was coming.

"We shouldn't presume it'll be bad though. The ancient Maya didn't. We can learn from their example. In the meantime, we have a beautiful day and the rest of this site to explore." Still holding my arm, he set off at a brisk pace, almost pulling me off my feet. Everyone scrambled to keep up with him while whispering among themselves, probably at the change in him. But no one wanted to be left behind. Only my eyes lingered on the cenote for as long as it was in view

Full of grisly secrets, how could anyone imagine it might yield a positive message of the future? You'd have to be very desperate. That reminded me of Kate and my mouth flattened into a hard line.

***

Early the next morning, April 7, I had a dream of being pregnant. I heard a drum and imagined it was a baby's heartbeat in my belly. I heard a horn and imagined it was a baby's wail in my ear. Then I heard more drums and more horns blending into an eerie melody that filled my body with primal energy.

But what woke me were Kate's soft movements. The creak of the bed as she rose. The padding of her bare feet across the floor. The click of the lock as she opened and closed the door to the hallway. A terrible certainty settled like ice in my stomach. The procedure, whatever it was, was happening now.

I felt I was still half dreaming as I launched myself after her. Despite my efforts to hurry, my feet were clumsy, sliding over cool tiles and then rough paving-stones, finally stumbling over tussocks of grass and arching tree-roots. I saw her and the other women as fluid shadows, impossibly nimble, first in the dim safety lights of the hacienda and other buildings and then in the much dimmer starlight beyond them.

My body was too sluggish to catch up to Kate, but I could follow the music. It grew louder as I penetrated the jungle, passing vine-clad mounds that might have been natural hills or forgotten ruins like Chichén Itzá once was. There was no way to tell. But this part of the estate wasn't entirely neglected. I was definitely following a well-worn path.

Fire suddenly glowed through the dense trees, as brilliant as sunrise. I was shading my eyes when I lurched into a clearing, marked out by torches. People crouched among them, cradling drums, or stood, blowing into horns that might have been conch shells. I was too dazzled to be sure. All I cared about was the glimpse of Kate's silver-blonde hair that I had before she disappeared into a round structure in the heart of the clearing.

Going after her, I found myself climbing several steps and passing between two pillars to reach a large raised platform. It was open to the sky and surrounded by a whole circle of pillars, each richly sculpted with images. Ixchel and Chaac stood out for me because they were everywhere, often very close together. I'd never seen them like that before, but I didn't have a chance to wonder what it meant.

All my concentration was on piercing the sweet-scented blue smoke draped over the middle of the platform like mist. I did see another ring of fire, this time burning in a series of stone braziers. I suspected they were burning incense too. It was strong enough to make my eyes water as I tried to move forward.

Female shadows teased me as I frantically looked for Kate. Then a voice, instantly recognizable as Dr. De Luna's, rose above the entrancing music and the crackling flames.

"Sisters! Conventional methods haven't worked for you, yet all the tests show you are capable of having a child. Let me tell you now that the universe has kept you waiting for a reason. It has been preparing you for this moment. Your presence here is an affirmation of that!"

There were many murmurs from within the smoke, but the women sounded dazed. Or drugged. It had to be something like that, I told myself. Kate wouldn't be out here otherwise. She wasn't crazy enough to believe in this nonsense. But my thudding heart suggested otherwise.

"Let me show you what you've been waiting for! Blood will open the way!" The director's voice rang out again and then there was a quick gasp of pain. Suddenly, the smoke began to swirl away. It lifted from the platform and hovered higher in the air. That was strange enough, but what followed was so bizarre I couldn't look away even to find Kate.

Dr. De Luna was visible now, holding a black obsidian knife, her bleeding tongue protruding from her lips. She licked them and then spat out a globule of blood. It arced away from her and fell into the glittering expanse of water before her. It was another cenote, about the same size as the one I'd seen at Chichén Itzá but much closer to the surface. The platform had been built around it.

The water, previously black as the director's knife except for shaky reflections of the flames, turned shockingly crimson and began to spiral, drawing the smoke down into it. The smoke vanished into the whirlpool, there was a moment of tranquility and then the whirlpool reversed itself, spinning the smoke back out.

But it was no longer smoke. Instead, it seemed to have become actual mist, striated with scarlet. It shrouded the platform again but was oddly translucent. When Dr. De Luna cried out, "The Vision Serpent awakes! The portal to the Otherworld opens!" I could see her. She was changing though. The mist was changing her.

It gave her height and age and majesty. Her upswept silvery hair became a serpent headdress. Her ears lengthened into jaguar ears. Her hands and feet transformed into jaguar paws. When she spoke next, her voice had changed as well. It was still smooth and calming but sounded older, grander, as if she had been honing it for centuries.

"Make your choice now, my sisters! Offer yourself for the future and you shall have what you desire!" That voice rippled outward and all the women swayed. I saw them ranged around the cenote, Kate among them. My heart jumped into my throat as the mist writhed over them like snakes. I had no idea what they were seeing, but, one by one, they turned toward the blood-red water and dove in.

"No!" I screamed when Kate vanished, leaving barely a ripple, but a hand over my mouth cut me off. My head jerked around and I saw him, the guide, although I barely recognized him. The mist had changed him too. Only his eyes were the same. He'd grown much taller, much younger. His nose had lengthened and scales covered his face. When he grinned at me, there were fangs in his mouth.

"I can't let you interrupt this time," he scolded me with dark humor. He held me easily with one arm as he held up something in his other hand. It was as long as his cane but looked more like an axe. Lifting me off my feet and striding forward, he cut through the mist that hung over the cenote.

Lightning sizzled from his axe and I recoiled in terror. But I couldn't get away. Brilliant white blinded me and burned my skin. I screamed again and this time he let me. When I could see once more, the mist had risen and become cloud, one patch of heavy grey cloud in an otherwise star-dominated sky. Right over the platform.

The director stepped in front of me. I hadn't seen her move. She took my face in her paws, gazing down at me almost tenderly. The serpent coiled around her forehead was more impassive.

"Nine months from this day, the world will change. On December 23, a new age will begin. A new race will be born. A better race, respectful of the gods, aware of their wisdom. You could be part of it. You have the potential. You heard the call. Join your sisters in the pool."

The voice, still majestic, was as intimate as a caress, but I shook my head violently. "No. No! I came for Kate. That's all."

"Are you sure about that, young lady?" breathed the guide in my ear, mocking me. "Why come for her when she hasn't been there for you? When she always puts her desires first? You don't like it. I've seen it."

"I love her!" I shouted, denying him, denying my own doubts. I was quaking with fear, but I'd remembered my anger. It made me brave enough to glare at her and then back at him. "You killed her. Killed all of them. All for some crazy idea of an apocalypse. Nothing's going to change. Not in a good way. It never does." I choked on a sob and stared at the cenote. It was barely moving.

"Too bad," murmured the director, releasing my face.

"So be it," pronounced the guide, throwing us both forward.

I hit the water first and then, a second later, his body hit mine. The double impact knocked most of the air from my lungs and propelled us deep into the frigid depths of the cenote. I struggled to swim but he still restrained me with his powerful arm. He pulled me around so we were facing each other as we sank.

His eyes, black as the blackest obsidian, locked onto mine and I saw a vision in them. The cloud bursting into a shower of rain. The women—*Kate!*— bobbing to the surface. Eyes and mouth open, drops falling into them. The women blinking, swallowing and smiling.

He blinked rapidly and new visions appeared. A new one with each blink. The women returning home with their partners. Kate leaving without me. Their bellies swelling as the months pass. All around the world, on one day, the women going into labor. The women cradling their new babies with their husbands beside them. Kate cradling her baby all alone.

I should have been happy, to know Kate would live, but it wasn't enough. Not like that. Not without me. I twisted in his grip but he shook his head at me. I mouthed "*Liar!*" and almost choked. He shook his head again, almost sadly, and then looked away from me. Following his eyes, I saw the women all around us, rising through the luminous red water.

Kate shot past but didn't see me, too focused on kicking her way to the surface. All the fight went out of me. I sagged under the guide's arm and he loosened it. Hope sparked in me. I thought he was letting me go.

But he was only freeing himself. Pointing his axe upward, some force lifted him past the swimming women. I reached for him, his arm, his leg, his ankle. But the suffocating embrace and the cold water had almost numbed me. I could barely move.

I lost sight of him and Kate and all the others long ago. But I am still falling.

2012AD

THE FIVE HILLS OF ICHCAANZIHO

By Jenny Ashford

Why am I doing this?

The thought was like a distant drumbeat in the back of Lucero's mind as he gently drew the needle from Sara's arm. He watched in fascinated horror as the clear liquid beaded like a perfect teardrop in the crook of her elbow. Shaking, he pulled the covers up to her chest. She stirred, briefly, and Lucero stepped back palming the syringe, but then she settled, her breathing becoming slow, deep and even. Lucero thought he could even see a slight smile on her lips, but that may have been wishful thinking. He leaned over and kissed her forehead, his stomach a tight knot. Lucero then tossed the syringe into the wastebasket near the bed, where two used needles lay blasphemously among crumpled tissues and empty soda cans.

Through the cracks in the vertical blinds, he could see the setting sun blazing across the Mediterranean, and the first fingers of cloud that signaled a storm to come.

He glanced over at Sara, and then at the
children, who all looked snug and peaceful beneath
their blankets. Their chests were still rising and falling
with calm regularity, their lungs clearly imagining
they had all the time in the world. Lucero plucked an
apple from the basket on the table and stepped out onto
the balcony.

The beach below was deserted, which seemed a
great shame. For some reason Lucero had hoped to see
hordes of humanity, gathering together at this
breathtaking vista, exalting in the glorious sunset, in
the sheer joy of being alive. He did not know precisely
why, but he was surprised by how fervently he wished
it—surprised by the depth of disappointment he felt
upon seeing the empty beach. He wanted to reach out
and pull the universe into his embrace, to covet it like a
jealous lover.

He did not know why he had come here. He
knew that this was the place Sara loved most, the place
where they had spent their honeymoon fifteen years
before. He tried to tell himself that this was the only
reason he had come, but the drumbeat in his head was
insistent. There had been vivid recurring dreams of an
endless series of pasts and futures that seemed to
contain some core of him. There had been plans,
research into painless poisons. And if he really
admitted it, there had been a distancing, as he closed
himself up and moved away from the charmed circle of
family. He did not know if Sara or his children had felt
it, but he most certainly had, and it had made these
past few months an agony in search of finality.

Lucero tossed the spent apple core onto the
beach, where a breeze covered it with sand. He turned
away from the darkening sky and trudged back

through the glass doors. The interior of the hotel room was cool but pleasant, lit only by a single sconce above the bed. The children sprawled peacefully, their dark hair mingling on their shared pillow, their mouths still taking in the air through the tiny pink o's of their lips. Sara still lay, hands folded over her chest. Lucero's heart clenched when he thought her life had faded away in his absence, but no, she still lived, though her breathing was so shallow that he could barely discern it. He pulled a chair alongside the bed and grasped her hand in his.

He could not believe that a few short hours ago, this woman and these children had been running along the beach outside, their shoes dangling from their fingers, their shadows dancing across the sands. The sound of their laughter as the waves lapped at their feet seemed to echo down the ages, captured in the threads of space for eternity. Their bodies now were so quiet seemingly incapable of anything so dynamic as sound or movement. The incongruity of their past and present states made Lucero feel hollow, unmoored from his own flesh.

For a moment Lucero found himself wondering if Sara would exist again, someday in a distant future, in a city built on the contingencies of the coming centuries. It was a bizarre idea seemingly coming from nowhere. The drumbeat in his head was becoming pronounced now, and it felt more and more as though some alien consciousness was working through him, propelling him to acts whose outcomes were repugnant, whose reasons were unclear to him. He thought he might perhaps be rationalizing what he suddenly realized was murder, and then he calmly considered the possibility that he might be crazy. He squeezed Sara's hand tighter.

He did not notice quite when it happened, but all at once he was aware of a strange silence in the room, a silence that he quickly attributed to the cessation of the sound of respiration from two sets of small lungs. The children were dead. He wanted to cry, bellow to the heavens, as the emotion welled up in him, but something between it and his skin acted as a barrier, and his outer shell remained unbroken. He felt as though he was inside a bottle. The sight of his two dead children—alive only seconds before, and looking no less alive now—tucked into their large hotel bed seemed academic, like an art installation.

Lucero heard a distant peal of thunder from outside, then a streak of lightning made the lamp above Sara's bed flicker like the stuttering illumination of a firefly. Before the purple ghost of the flash had left his eyes, the hand he held went subtly limp, and Sara's last breath escaped her lips like the ebbing of the tide on a faraway shore.

***

Kay met Terry on the stairs of their apartment building; she was walking down, he was walking up. The stairwell was lit by a single smudged bulb behind a small metal cage.

"Are you sure this is the best way?" Terry's brow was furrowed, leaving his dark eyes nothing but pools of shadow.

Kay crossed her arms across her chest feeling a sudden chill. "Is there really a best way? It's the best way we could come up with."

Terry nodded soberly. "I just hope everyone's asleep."

"Well, it can't be helped if they're not." Kay's eyes were outlined in black, the result of not having slept for several days. Without another word, she descended to the landing and pushed the bar on the red door that led to the boiler room. Terry followed, peering over his shoulder.

When they emerged into the stairwell again, fifteen minutes later, they were both shaking. The dimness and the damp and the complete silence made the recesses of the building feel like a mausoleum. Neither of them spoke as they ascended one flight to ground level, then made their escape through the rear fire door.

The streets of Chetumal were empty at this hour, and though there was no need to hurry, Kay and Terry nonetheless strode swiftly away from the building they'd both called home for nearly a decade. Terry glanced back peering up at the darkened windows. "What about Mrs. Alvarez, she's always up late reading..."

"Terry, stop. It's too late now." Kay's old blue Ford was parked around the corner, and she unlocked it. They got in and closed the doors, breathing hard.

After a few moments of staring straight ahead through the windshield, Kay reached into her bag and pulled out a pack of cigarettes. She offered one to Terry, but he shook his head. Kay lit up and puffed in silence, filling the car with a sharp gray smog. She did not roll down the windows, and Terry did not ask her to.

Their building was no longer in sight, but Terry still stared out the window in its general direction as if he'd be able to witness the rooms filling with carbon monoxide, see the lives snuffed out behind the dark windows. "We just killed fifty-seven people." His voice was as soft as a breath.

Kay stubbed out her cigarette and lit another. "It doesn't matter now, Terry. You know that."

"I know." He glanced over at her, his wide face a mask floating in the smoke. "Should we do more, then? I mean, we'd be doing them a mercy."

Kay's chin began to tremble, but she sniffed and got a hold of herself. "It was hard enough just doing this, Terry. I wish I could do more."

He nodded again. Another long moment passed while Kay finished her second cigarette and then reached out with an unsteady hand to start the car. Its engine roared to life, and Terry winced. She maneuvered through the empty streets, not speaking until after she had driven clear of Chetumal and exited onto the Carretera del Mundo Maya, heading toward Mérida.

"Do we know how to get in touch with Lucero?" she asked.

Terry pulled a slip of paper out of his wallet. "I have his cell phone number here. I suppose I'll wait until morning to call him."

"No, do it now," Kay said, squinting after the Ford's too-bright headlights. "I have a strange feeling that there might be problems."

Terry's head snapped up. "Problems?"

"You mean you don't feel it?"

"I don't know." He played absently with the buttons on his phone. "Maybe. You think Lucero won't come?"

"He has to come. I just have...other concerns. We'll call him and see what he says."

"All right." Terry held the slip of paper up to the light, then dialed the number.

***

Lucero had packed his things and now sat staring absently at his suitcase. Sara and the children were motionless shapes beneath the white sheets, and Lucero tried his best not to look at them. The night had passed almost without his being aware of it and dawn was approaching. He could not yet see the first rays of sunlight sparkling upon the waves of the Mediterranean, but he could still hear the whispered roar of waters as they pounded the beach beyond his window.

He had no idea what his next move should be; it occurred to him that he should leave before anyone became suspicious, but for some reason he felt little fear that his deed would be discovered. He still was not sure why he had done it and his heart ached, but now he felt a strange calm also, as if everything would be taken care of if he could only be patient for a little longer.

His cell phone rang, loudly, but it did not startle him. Perhaps, he mused, he had been expecting it. Moving like a man in a dream, he reached into his pocket and put the tiny phone to his ear. He listened.

"Is this Lucero?" The voice on the other end was gritty, earthy, with an accent that suggested Mexico or Central America.

"Yes."

A pause. "Do you know what day it is tomorrow?"

Lucero was taken aback momentarily. "I..." he stuttered. "It's December twenty-first, isn't it?"

There was another pause, then a sigh. It sounded as though the man had covered the phone with his hand; his voice was muffled as he spoke to someone on his end. After a moment his words filled Lucero's ear again. "You have to come to Mérida, do you understand? You must come immediately."

"I killed my family." Lucero hadn't meant to say it like that, but until he had spoken aloud he hadn't realized how badly he needed to confess it. His eyes filled with tears. "I don't know why I did it. What's happening to me?"

"It's all right, Lucero. You did the right thing." More muffled voices. "What you need to do now is catch the first flight to Mérida, okay? Where are you now?"

Lucero looked around the hotel room, for a second unable to remember where he was. Then it came to him. "Amalfi Coast. Italy."

The man blew air loudly between his lips. "All right. You're far away, but you can still make it if you hurry. Do you know where Mérida is?"

The name conjured up barely remembered visions in Lucero's mind. "I...can't remember."

"It's on the Yucatan Peninsula, Lucero, you know where that is? Get a flight to the Manuel Crescencio Rejon International Airport, right? We'll pick you up and tell you what you have to do."

"We?"

"That's not important now. You have to get here before tomorrow. Don't worry about anything else, just get here as soon as you can. Call me when you've arrived. My name's Terry."

"All right, Terry." Lucero hung up the phone. Driven by some internal mechanism he picked up his suitcase and left the hotel room without once looking back at the three bodies he left in his wake.

***

"Hail Itzam Cab Ain!" The follower, a man in fatigues with blond dreadlocks, pressed an object into Delia's hand. When Delia opened her fingers, she saw that it was a tiny gold idol, a figure of a woman with a crocodile head. Emotion welled up within her, but she suppressed it with a force born of long practice. "Thank you, Marcus," she said, and laid her hand upon his shoulder. He closed his eyes and smiled, as if her touch had conferred the understanding of the ages upon him in one bright flash. Then he bowed his head, and drank from the cup of green liquid in front of him. The smile remained on his face as he stretched out on the floor and crossed his hands upon his chest, waiting for the end.

Delia watched the others as they drank, none hesitating in the slightest, and a wave of admiration for them managed to override her detachment. They were really the most extraordinary creatures when they wanted to be. She looked again at the small gold idol in her hand. It was beautifully made; Marcus had been something of a genius in the art of shaping metals. It was a shame he would make nothing else; that everything he had made would soon disappear forever. She would keep this trinket, though, with its charming crocodilian features. It was sentimentality, she knew, but what harm was there?

She sat in the farmhouse until the last of her followers had fallen still; she felt she owed them that much. The wide windows looked out upon a mountain vista capped with cotton white clouds, and Delia spent a long moment in contemplation of the lives that had met their dignified finish beneath this sky. Then she rose and made her way outside.

A little more than an hour later, Delia slid her tortoiseshell sunglasses up onto her head and took an enormous bite of her second hamburger, absently wiping mustard from her chin. The sky was growing dark, but the sound and rubber smell of engines racing down the freeway seemed to be growing exponentially. Chewing, she watched the endless parade of winter travelers milling like bees around the rest stop's dubious nectar of snack foods and filthy conveniences. Most of them were clad in khaki shorts and t-shirts advertising mountain lodges; even though it was nearly Christmas, southern California was sweltering.

Wolfing down the last of her food and licking her fingers, Delia tossed the paper wrappers in the trash and got up from the picnic table, stretching her stiffening muscles. She hated long drives, but she hated flying even more; being more than a few feet above the ground made her intensely uncomfortable. She tried to console herself by thinking that this road trip was the last one she'd be taking for a very long time, but she was still reluctant to fold her lithe limbs into her battered tin can on wheels. At last she steeled herself, and drifted to her car, starting it with a roar. The little gold crocodile statue grinned at her from its perch on the dashboard, and she returned its cheery expression.

As she maneuvered out of the rest stop, she felt a wave of pity for the poor creatures in their straw hats and sandals, for their complete lack of awareness of impending events. She glanced back at them in her rearview mirror, but then made herself focus on the road ahead. It was certainly unfortunate that these hapless people might be terrified and perhaps suffer needlessly, but she had done her part for those closest to her. She couldn't spare everyone. Time was running out, and she had to be on the move.

The sun warmed her skin through the windshield and she soaked up the rays, feeling her body temperature rising pleasantly. Her brain was a boiling mass of emotions, from anxiety to elation to sorrow for all that she had left behind. Idly, she wondered if anyone had stumbled upon the bodies yet, if police had been alerted, if even now yellow crime scene tape was bring strung around the perimeter of the farmhouse that served as a mass grave for her followers. She felt her mouth twisting into a smirk at the thought of the reports that would doubtlessly dominate the evening newscasts. Scene of unbelievable horror, they would say, faces held in mock sobriety. An American Jonestown. Perhaps there would even be out-of-focus photographs of her elusive form flashed upon the screen, descriptions of the one who had got away, the one who was likely responsible.

Delia hoped, for the sake of her disciples, that their bodies had not been found, that they would rest quietly in their mountain retreat until the coming cataclysm wiped their deaths from the historical record, made them meaningless, nonexistent, never-existent. Delia wished this so passionately that she nearly crushed the steering wheel between her hands.

***

Lucero had managed to secure a seat on a flight to New York, then on a connecting flight to Mérida, but both planes were packed to capacity, and even in first class he felt oppressed by the closeness of the other travelers. It seemed as though every spare niche in the aircraft was crammed with gaily wrapped packages, and Lucero had to look away from their festive physicality, suspecting they would never be opened. Instead he stared out the window at the clouds cruising by far below.

Some interminable amount of time later, he was crossing the terminal of Manuel Crescencio Rejon International Airport when his cell phone rang again, this time startling him so severely that he nearly screamed. Several passengers looked at him oddly, and he gave them a smile he hoped looked reassuring, fishing the phone from his pocket. Without looking at the number, he put it to his ear. "Yes?"

"Hello, Lucero." A woman's voice now, speaking English with a thicker accent than Terry's. Even though Lucero had never heard this particular voice before, it seemed intimately familiar. "We're in the blue Taurus, right out the doors past the leftmost baggage claim. Are you doing all right?" The concern in the woman's voice made Lucero relax.

"Yes. I think so. But I still don't know what's going on."

A long pause. "Well, we'll sort that out as soon as you get here." The phone crackled as a plane rumbled close overhead. "I've reserved rooms at the Villa, only a few blocks from Main Square."

"Thank you." Lucero's voice was hoarse as he rang off. He didn't like this nervousness, this feeling

that everyone seemed to be part of an intricate plot that
he knew nothing about. To take his mind away, he
focused on the relief of being off the cramped plane
and in a country that he'd always wanted to visit but
had never got around to. When he stepped out through
the sliding doors of the terminal and into the waning
sunlight, the sky and earth and trees seemed to reach
down and cradle him in warmth, in eternal familiarity.

He spotted the car right away, and jogged over
to it, his suitcase bumping against his thigh. As he slid
into the back seat, he took in the pair in the front. A
man and woman whose voices had come to him when
his life had taken its darkest turn, when he most
needed rescue. The man driving, presumably Terry,
was burly and broad featured, with leathery skin and a
tumble of black curls. The woman, who turned and
introduced herself as Kay, was willowy, delicate, her
long dark hair shot through with strands of reddish
gold. She smiled, though her brow was furrowed with
concern. "It's nice to see you, despite the
circumstances," she said. Her big eyes blinked as she
considered him. "You really don't know why you're
here or what's happening, do you?"

Lucero shook his head, feeling a vague sense of
shame, as though he had disappointed her.

She glanced over at Terry, who simply stared
out the windshield as he pulled into the seething snarl
of traffic surrounding the airport exit. "It's rather
difficult to explain..."

"Why did I kill my Sara?" Lucero asked, the
enormity of his deed suddenly assaulting him anew,
leaving his chest feeling so tight he thought it might
implode. "Do you know why I did that?"

Terry flicked a glance at him in the rearview mirror. "We also killed those nearest to us. Believe me, it was the merciful thing."

Kay turned awkwardly in the passenger seat. "Oh Lucero, how terrible for you not to remember. This has never happened before, not in all the years..." She drifted off again, her beautiful, airy face a mask of consternation.

Terry made a turn, narrowly missing an old man on a bicycle. "Maybe it would be better to just tell him outright," he said, casting a sidelong look at Kay.

Lucero looked first at Terry and then at Kay, feeling that they were opposites and yet somehow still one. They seemed much larger than they appeared, as though they both had powerful magnetic fields emanating from their bodies. He was sweating beneath his clothes, desperate for some shred of understanding, of information.

Kay turned toward the front of the car again. "Maybe we should wait for Delia. Wait until we're all together."

"What for?"

"I don't know. Maybe Delia would be better at telling him."

Terry nodded slowly. "Maybe."

"Who is Delia and what is she supposed to tell me?" Lucero asked, feeling peevish but not wanting to sound so.

They glanced at each other again, their eyes wide in shared conspiracy. Kay did not seem to want to answer, but Terry apparently took pity on him. "Delia is Itzam Cab Ain," he said, nosing the car through the dusty streets. "She is the eater of the futures."

**

It was nearly evening when they arrived at the hotel. It was an imposing structure, all arches and orange stucco, two stories presiding over a surrounding lake of green grass and white winter blossoms. Kay and Terry had been nothing but friendly during the remainder of the trip, but Lucero was still frustrated by their reluctance to talk more. They checked into the hotel and had a valet take Lucero's bag up to his room; the two of them evidently had no luggage, which disturbed Lucero immensely. The three of them then sat on the veranda of the attached restaurant, drinking coffee; Kay and Terry did not ignore him, but they mostly spoke between themselves. The rhythm of their voices was strangely soothing, like wind through wheat fields.

Lucero was just beginning to come to terms with the surreal turn his life had taken, and was beginning to accept the fact that he may never completely understand what was happening to him, when he glanced up and out across the grass, and there, he knew, was Delia.

Her voluptuous figure swayed beneath a green silk caftan, and her eyes were hidden by dark glasses despite the approaching night. She moved neither gracefully or clumsily; her motion was inevitable. For a moment she too seemed enormous, slithering, and the aura of power streamed from her in thick verdant waves. As Lucero stared, the lawn and street below suddenly seemed to swim, and Delia's looming frame looked large enough to swallow the world. Lucero gripped the edges of the table to anchor himself in reality.

Delia slid into a chair opposite him, taking off her glasses and studying him with flat yellowish eyes. Without preamble she said, "Are you going to be able to do this, Lucero?"

He was frozen, prey before a hungry predator. Cold seemed to radiate from her like pale blue light.

Before he could stammer out an answer, Kay swooped in. "Delia, he doesn't know."

She almost growled as her head whipped to confront Kay. "Doesn't know? How can he not know?"

Kay shrugged, clearly not intimidated by Delia at all. "Stranger things have happened, I suppose."

Delia's mouth twisted and she almost looked amused. Her gaze fell on Lucero again. "Bolon Dzacab," she said.

Lucero stared at her, then at the others, wondering if this was all some elaborate joke. "What?"

Delia sat back in her chair, her tongue flicking across her lips. "Very interesting. I wonder why he's forgotten."

Terry sipped from his coffee cup. "He had a wife. Children," he said.

At the mention of his family, Lucero stiffened. "What have they got to do with anything?" It suddenly occurred to him that he had confessed to killing Sara and the girls, that if Kay and Terry wanted to, they could turn him in. Why had he told them? They were clearly not going to help him; they were looking at him like he was a bug under a microscope.

Delia was nodding, her eyes glinting knowingly. "Hm, yes. It never pays to get too close to them. Now we see why."

"What are you talking about?" Lucero was gripping the handle of his cup so hard that he thought he heard the ceramic crack. "Tell me what's going on!" He supposed he could just get up and leave, but where would he go? He was a murderer in an unfamiliar country. It would only be a matter of time before he was caught.

Kay took his hand in hers, and though his first instinct was to pull away, she stroked his fingers gently until he submitted. "We're sorry about this, Lucero," she said, and her voice was honeyed, sky-blue spring. "It's just that this is so unusual. Normally when a rebirth comes around, we're all...on the same page, as it were." She smiled weakly.

"Rebirth?" Lucero whispered.

Delia put her palms flat upon the table top. "Basically the situation is this," she said. "Tomorrow is the last day before the rebirth of the world, the start of a new five-millennial age. We've been presiding over these rebirths for..."

"Forever," Terry said, and the three of them laughed.

"As good as," Delia said. "Now, when the cataclysm begins..."

"The what?"

Delia sighed. "For heaven's sake, Lucero, we haven't got much time here. Just pipe down and I'll tell you what you need to know. As I said, it all goes down tomorrow, precisely at dawn. It will happen whether or not we are here to oversee it, but if we were not here for some reason..."

"It wouldn't be a rebirth," Kay broke in quietly. "It would be the end. The true end."

"Precisely." A waiter hovered into view, and Delia ordered more coffee and an almond pastry before sending him away with a flick of her oddly claw like hand. Then she pointed a finger at Lucero. "You, Bolon Dzacab, have the most important duty of all. It will probably all come back to you when the Five Hills rise up again, but in a nutshell you are the one who chooses the next future, the next five-millennial existence. Understand?"

Lucero stared hard into her face, looking for some clue that she was teasing him, winding him up. But she only blinked matter-of-factly; Kay and Terry looked on with serious and slightly anxious expressions. After a moment he laughed, a burbling cackle that startled him as it came out of his mouth. "I understand that you're all crazy," he said.

Delia leaned forward, her features blazing intently. "Listen to me. Deep down you know what I'm saying is true. It's inside you, Lucero. You have lived many lifetimes, in many different bodies, always waiting for this day to come. Even when you first got here, you thought you had been here before, didn't you?"

Lucero turned away trying to hide his shocked expression. She smiled. "And you've been having dreams— dreams of living as other people, in other times. But they aren't dreams, Lucero. You did live them. You can remember if you try."

Lucero didn't want to try, didn't want to feel as though these three strange people knew more about him than he knew about himself. What were they doing to him, reminding him of visions he wanted forgotten? Were they somehow controlling his thoughts even now? Had they been the ones who made him kill Sara and the girls? His hands shook.

Delia sighed. "We're not getting anywhere." She peered out over the railing, taking in the city

below as if some answer could perhaps be found there.
Evening had fallen fully upon Mérida, and though the
night was unseasonably cool, the throngs of people and
the rush of traffic had barely dissipated. From the
veranda the city lights seemed to go on forever, the
glowing speckles of modernity a thin covering over the
black unknown seething beneath. Lucero thought again
of how he could leap from the veranda, disappear into
the night among strangers and find some way of
escaping this country. As though she had read his
mind, Delia placed her hand gently but firmly upon his
arm. "Let's go up to our rooms. Maybe a rest will put
you in a better frame of mind," she said.

"We could all use a rest, I think," said Terry.

"Big day tomorrow," said Kay, and then
laughed awkwardly and looked down at her hands.

"Lucero? You'll be all right, won't you?" Delia's
yellow gaze was hard, distrustful, but not without
kindness.

Lucero brought his trembling cup to his lips and
drained the coffee from it. His brain was a hive of
confusion. His entire being had become fragmented
and now struggled to reassemble itself. "I'll...be all
right," he said, though he choked upon the words. "I
need to sleep."

"Of course you do." Delia watched him as he
rose unsteadily to his feet. She and the two others
followed close at his heels as he entered the hotel, and
Lucero got the distinct impression that they were
blocking his escape routes. He winced at the stifling
heat in the lobby, hitting him full in the face after the
pleasant coolness outdoors. He was aware that people
seemed to be staring at him, and for a panicked
moment he was sure they knew who he was, that the

murders of his wife and children were stamped upon his flesh. Despite this, he was tempted to plead for help with his eyes. *Get me away from here*, he wanted to say, hoping that someone would intervene and push aside these insane people. But he did nothing of the sort. He simply shuffled to the elevator in the midst of his group of jailers, and ascended to the fifth floor.

***

Delia's eyes sprang open in the darkness, every cell of her body seeming to quiver. She did not know exactly what time it was, but she had a feeling that in some sense it was already too late.

She had not meant to fall asleep tonight, and for the first few hours after the four had retired to their rooms, she had lay on her belly across the bed, keeping perfectly still, watching the lights of Mérida winking out one by one. But eventually the stress of the past days and the forced languor of the long drive had caught up to her, and she drifted off.

Now, though, she knew something was wrong. She slid out of bed, listening at the walls. Terry and Kay could be heard moving around their room, apparently as reluctant to sleep as she. But from Lucero's room was only silence. Delia sighed heavily. She had known something like this might happen, but she hadn't wanted to force the issue with Lucero by making him stay in the room with her. She knew in some sense he already felt that, but she also knew that in his heart of hearts he knew what he was and what he needed to do. She had just been hoping that this realization would come to him before his panicky

human veneer could override the godly duty residing
in his very genes. Evidently this had not happened.

Delia shrugged into her clothes, annoyed at
Lucero and herself for not being able to convince him.
A glance at the bedside clock revealed the time to be
nearing 3 a.m. There was still time to find Lucero
before events began to unfold in earnest; she did not
know how long ago he had absconded, but he was in a
strange city, and likely hadn't gotten far. As she
stepped out into the hallway of the hotel she saw that
Kay and Terry were emerging also, matching
expressions of exhaustion tainting their lovely brown
faces.

Without a word, the three formed a small
huddle and moved as one toward the elevator.

***

Lucero was bleary-eyed but curiously wide
awake. He had no idea where he was or where he
thought he was going; he only knew he had to get away
from those people, from everything he'd done. The
sunrise was still more than an hour off, but a soft
pinkish glow had begun to emanate from beyond the
horizon, garlanding the edges of the modern buildings
with a clear, liquid light. He stopped a moment and
stared at the fading stars. He felt that he was at a
crossroads, an ending, yes, but perhaps also a
beginning.

Shaking himself out of the strange visions that
had started to nibble at the corners of his
consciousness, he set off walking down the side of a
deserted road that led out of Mérida and toward the
main highway. Perhaps when the sun came up he could

hitchhike, find someone who could help him get back home, although he wasn't sure he knew where that was anymore. With falling spirits he realized that he could never go back there anyway; he was a marked man.

Lucero wasn't sure how long he had been walking, but the light in the sky had begun to change from pink to orange. He realized he felt something happening to the ground beneath his feet. For a time he kept walking, resolutely, unwilling to acknowledge the sensation, but a few more steps told him he could no longer ignore it. He stopped and looked around, his heart fluttering. Was it an earthquake? It certainly felt like that, but there was also something else, some harmonic tone just beyond the threshold of hearing. Lucero twisted and turned, wildly, looking for something or someone who could explain what was happening, but the roads around him were still deserted at this time of the morning.

A sudden jolt sent him flying, and he landed with a painful thud on his right side. Cradling his arm he sat up, feeling the ground trembling beneath him, and then there was another jolt, several times more powerful than the last, that rattled his bones against the inside of his skin. He tried to stand but the earth no longer felt solid, and he slipped to the ground, terrified and covered in mud. As he sat on the ground, wondering at its treachery and trying to think of a way out of his predicament, he thought he saw in the darkness an enormous snake making its way like a lightning strike toward him. He recoiled before realizing that what he had seen was actually something far worse than a snake; it was an enormous crack in the earth, zigzagging at him almost purposefully, like a crooked-mouthed beast aiming to swallow him whole.

He screamed and rolled aside, feeling the crack rocket past him, and then the harmonic sound seemed to grow many times louder, as if it emanated from the very core of the earth and was released by the opening of the ground.

And then there was another sound, one which he had heard many times but in this context seemed particularly out of place; it was the roar of a nearby ocean. The moment he heard the mysterious shush of the waves he smelled them also, a deep salty smell that seemed to hold all of the secrets of humankind to its black breast, seemed to hide their hopes in its unfathomable depths. As he stared transfixed into the gigantic crack in the earth that had narrowly missed eating him alive, he saw the waters climbing the walls of the chasm, rushing headlong toward the surface.

The ocean was nearly to the lip of the fissure when Lucero felt a light brush of a breeze across his cheek, and in the dawning light a shadow fell across him. Gazing upward, he thought perhaps he had died without realizing and now languished in the care of the angels, though it was Kay's face that hung above him. "There you are," she seemed to say, though her words meshed with the harmonies, making them difficult to discern. She seemed to encompass the entire firmament, a beautiful countenance made of stars and galaxies and darkness. It seemed that she smiled at him, and he felt as though he smiled back, and then he remembered nothing for a little while.

***

When Lucero awoke, he found himself standing in the middle of a large cobbled square, the center of

the city of Mérida, with empty benches watching like
sentinels from the sidelines. The ground still shook,
the sounds of music and rushing water still filled his
ears, but now he felt strangely calm, as if his body was
no longer his own, as if he was watching this happen
from somewhere very far away. He glanced to his left
and his right and saw them, Kay and Terry and Delia,
and they looked the same but also somehow different;
lighter, less defined. Lucero closed his eyes, feeling a
chill breeze whispering across his face. Even with his
eyes closed, Lucero knew that lightning had begun to
arc across the sky; he could feel the hairs on his body
standing up with the electricity. The wildness of the
feeling excited him; he felt some affinity with the
lightning, thought of it as a brother element. The
visions that had haunted him for as long as he could
remember came fast now, flashing by in the red-black
space behind his eyes, but for some reason they no
longer caused him any fear. He opened his eyes.

The ground continued to shake, and somewhere
far away he heard people shouting, screams of anguish.
This made him apprehensive for a moment, and he
glanced at the others to gauge their reactions, but their
expressions were stoic. Delia gave his hand a cursory
squeeze, as if to tell him that things were exactly as
they should be, and he relaxed back into his detached
state.

More great cracks began to appear, branching
across the paving stones in patterns mimicking the
forking of lightning across the still-dim sky, and then
the ocean came boiling up from the depths of the
planet, steaming waters tipped with foaming white
caps, angry and insatiable. Lucero watched the levels
rise, feeling as though his entire body was surging with

light and power. He then turned fully to his
kidnappers, his compatriots.

Kay seemed to be growing, yet at the same time
becoming less present, more ethereal, her molecules
dissolving into the surrounding air. After a few
moments all he could see of her was her light, solemn
face and her outstretched arms like enormous blue
wings encompassing the atmosphere beneath their
shelter.

Terry was also growing, but he appeared to be
growing darker, bulkier, spreading himself even wider
as he sank into the yielding dirt. His strong features
seemed stamped in the very surface of the emerging
soil, an eyebrow or a smirk caught in the coincidental
patterns of the trembling earth.

Delia was not disintegrating into the
atmosphere the way the others were, but she was
nonetheless getting larger, her limbs becoming shorter
and more muscular, her face protruding forward, her
nose becoming a pointed snout, her flesh becoming
hard and plated. From the position she adopted, lying
on her belly with her powerful tail flicking behind her,
she stared up at Lucero with the same golden reptile
eyes that had considered him from beneath her
tortoiseshell sunglasses. He wondered idly what he
looked like to her now, whether the electricity coursing
through his veins was making of him a glowing,
sizzling figure of forking limbs and burning eye.

The cracks in the ground before them became
chasms, and through the paving and metal of modern
Mérida rose the ancient city of Ichcaanziho, which
always lay in wait, the past bubbling endlessly beneath
the present. The sound of the sky and the earth
collapsing and separating was deafening, drowning out

the cries of any humans who were still alive to witness it. The veneer of Mérida fell easily away as though it was made of paper, a cardboard city, and through its ruins rose the five hills of Ichcaanziho, green and lush with vegetation that smothered one with the scent of persistent life, cyclical life, that died and died again only to be reborn ever after, resilient, stubborn, immortal.

Kay with her cape of blue held the sky above like curtains, while Terry below them served as the stage upon which to act. The sun was coming up through the clouds, its bright disc just visible behind the five hills; it signified day one, the resetting, the rebirth.

The water had just begun to spill over the cracks, and rushed to fill the flat land in gobbling torrents. Lucero peered down at his dampening shoes, and then at Delia's crocodile form, which was so large that her eyeline was nearly level with his chest. She blinked at him, a gesture of assent, of encouragement. Lucero hesitated for a moment only, the last vestige of his human form making its uncertainty felt. Then he let go, allowing the blazing divinity he'd always harbored in the recesses of his soul to come forward and do its sacred duty. Taking one last look at the silhouette of the five hills stretching up into the brightening sky, he began to ascend the leftmost hill, with Delia dragging along close behind.

At the apex of the hill, Lucero stopped to take in a scene he would not lay eyes on for another five millennia or more. The sky was black above the sunrise, and the wings of Kay's cape had become a whirling vortex of even blacker mass, like storm clouds coughed up from the mouth of Xibalba itself. Rain was

falling in great buckets, adding more water to the
oceans that rose from the cracks in the earth. Very
soon the five hills were small, evenly spaced islands in
a vast and endless sea that heaved ever upward as the
rainwater battered its surface.

By the glow of his own inner fire, Lucero could
make out the temple in the center of the hill, a great
tree with branches reaching toward the heavens, its
trunk as thick as a thousand men. The tips of the
stretching fingers nearly touched those of the tree on
the next hill, forming a broken web of wood and leaf.

Lucero approached the temple, hearing Delia's
claws parting the grass behind him. The tree hung
heavy with round fruits that glinted like silvery jewels,
like diamonds, as his light neared it, and within each
fist-sized fruit was the cycling flicker of possibility. He
felt his eyes burning in their sockets as he
contemplated the fruits nearest to him, the lives and
fates playing out upon their surfaces. They were all so
beautiful, and all seemed to whisper to him, their
glittering shine flashing at him like a saucy wink. *We
are the future*, they all seemed to say. *It is we you must
choose, we who must live.*

Lucero felt a twinge of hesitation again, an ache
of regret; the human shell was apparently not so easily
cast aside. The centuries he had just lived through were
gone forever; they were not anywhere here, hanging
full and ripe from any of the five trees. Sara was not
here. The existence of every person he had ever been
and known was erased; with the new fruit he picked,
history would be rewritten, and there was no one save
himself and his compatriots who would remember that
there had ever been other eras, other cycles,
overlapping endlessly in the same fold in time. In

another 5200 years he would stand here again, the future he picked now vanished beneath the waves of the great sea.

Was it as pointless as it all seemed? Was the fact of humans' existence in any time important if after mere millennia it was all snatched away, subsumed, utterly replaced and forgotten?

Delia clacked her jaws behind him, regarding him with her yellow eyes. She was growing impatient, but he could also see understanding in her reptilian gaze. Lucero supposed it was not for him to question his duty to the great wheel of the universe, the cycle of existence. What difference did it make, in the end, which future he chose? Whichever fruit he plucked would guarantee sorrow and tragedy. But also there would be joy, hope, happiness, love, mercy—for wasn't that also the way of the human, the inevitable by-product?

Delia seemed to smile at him, as though she had read his thoughts and was glad to see that he finally understood. Then again, Delia's crocodile form always seemed to be smiling.

Lucero plucked a shimmering silver fruit from a high branch near the center of the temple, and after only a moment's contemplation of the future it contained, he tossed it to Delia, who caught it handily between her open jaws, and swallowed it with obvious relish.

Kay and Terry were instantly beside him again, their human forms still wavering around the edges. They touched his face, murmured congratulations.

Feeling as though a great weight had been lifted from his shoulders, feeling the anticipation of his three friends in godhood, Lucero stepped back from the tree,

waiting for the waters to subside, waiting for the sun
to rise, waiting for the next future to begin.

2012AD

Discovery

By Jason Colavito

Beware the places dark and green
Where writhe the mysteries unseen
Under leaf and bush untrod.

- QUINTUS SEPTIMIUS

A.D. 217

(Thompson translation)

Professor DeQuin bolted up from his desk and slapped his head in recognition that he had forgotten that he had a class this hour. He grabbed the briefcase where he kept his lecture notes, ran out of the faculty building, and sprinted across the Marius University campus. DeQuin chided himself for being so absent-minded; it was not his usual style. He could not recall the last time he had been late for a class, but neither could he remember the last time he had been privy to such a momentous discovery.

He rushed into a cheaply-built annex that housed additional classrooms for departments not allocated enough space in the more comfortable science building proper. His students were in the classroom, already fidgeting and talking loudly in his absence. One particularly dull student was loudly asserting the five minute rule, and threatening to walk out if the professor did not show soon. DeQuin walked to the front of the room and called for quiet.

"I have an important announcement regarding class today," DeQuin said. "I know how much you were all looking forward to my lecture on anthropomorphosis in pre-Christian mythology. . ." Polite laughter echoed from the students. ". . .but due to some unforeseen events, we will not have a lecture today." One student cheered loudly, and others murmured and mumbled their relief beneath their breath.

The students stood to leave, but DeQuin called them back. "Just because I'm not lecturing today does not mean that you don't have an assignment. I want you all to go to the Hatcher book and pick two of the culture areas we've studied and write a two-page comparison of their apocalyptic myths, due Friday-- Ragnorak, the Book of Revelations, the appearance of Kalki, and so on. Since it's near the end of the semester, studying the end times seems like an appropriate task." The kids groaned, and one raised his hand.

"Can we do the Mayan calendar? You know, the 2012 apocalypse?"

"Well, I'd rather you didn't. That's a mostly modern extrapolation of the fact that the Mayan calendar ends a cycle on December 21, 2012. I believe it was a modern psychic or hippie who invented the end of the world scenario off of that. You might have better luck researching the Aztec myth of the five suns."

Weighted with their assignments, the students decamped for greener pastures.

With the annoyance of the undergraduates safely disposed, DeQuin rummaged in his briefcase for a blank sheet of paper. He scrawled in thick marker "Prof. DeQuin's classes are canceled today," and he hung the sign on the classroom door with a piece of electrical tape clandestinely removed from the janitorial closet. He snapped the briefcase shut and hurried back to his office. He did not want to be bothered today.

***

Back in his office, he locked the door and sat down at his cluttered desk. He swept aside some interoffice memos and assorted collegiate detritus so he would have a space to study the object. It had come in the mail not two hours ago, and it filled him with awe and wonder. The letter attached to it made it doubly precious.

It was not the original artifact dug from the ground of course; such things could not be removed from Costa Rica legally without many permits; it was instead a cast. DeQuin carefully fingered the small plaster copy of what in the original was a stone artifact, and he looked at its every crevice underneath a powerful magnifying glass. He could tell that plainly this object was only part of a larger sculpture, now lost, that must have at one time been magnificent. One side, presumably the front, had a geometric pattern of repeating shapes, very regular in form and style, almost Mediterranean, possibly Minoan, in form. The other side showed only part of a mythological creature whose full features could only be guessed. Accompanying photographs showed the color and patina of the original, and even in pictures, the antiquity of the object was obvious.

DeQuin shuddered with joy. If this was what he thought it was, then quite possibly it could prove his long-held assertion that the Minoans or Mycenaean's, or maybe their predecessors, had circumnavigated the world. He was sure of it now, for the piece of plaster he held in his hand bore words written in the unmistakable archaic Greek known in written form as Linear B.

The professor turned to the letter, written by Amanda Ungbon, one of his more distinguished former students. She was spending the semester doing anthropological studies in Central America, but DeQuin was sure that she would be a great anthropologist in the mold of Boaz or Trigger. When she had telephoned him last week about a newly-discovered tribe, he was filled with a childlike thrill of discovery. Now she wrote with more details, and the artifact. He re-read her letter again:

***

San Pedro, April 5, 2010
Prof. DeQuin -

First of all, how have you been? I'm so sorry that you were stuck teaching intro level cultural anthro again this semester. Dean Francesco must really not like you much. Anyway, Costa Rica has been an amazing experience. Some of the tribes I've encountered here appear to have undergone almost no cultural evolution since the Spanish Conquest. But that's not why I'm writing. I want to tell you more about the new tribe I started to tell you about when I called you the other day.

Last week I sneaked along to El Lugar de Noche Negra with Dr. Hernández from the Universidad de Costa Rica. The area is approximately 27 miles outside the small village of Santa Maria de los Caballos. El Lugar seems at first to be an empty area devoid of past or present life, but el doctor Hernández took us to a site that his team has just found. He was upset that I stowed away, but when we got there he warmed up. You know Dr. Hernández. He's an expert in pre-Mayan cultures and worked on the Olmec calendar that the Mayans adopted. The Olmecs up in Mexico had a 52-year cycle with years of 360 days, as opposed to the Maya with their interlocking 260 day *tzolk'in* calendar and the Long Count of 52 years. So, the idea is that the Mayans were inspired by the Olmec, and Dr. H. thinks the Olmecs may have inherited the calendar from a pre-Olmec culture from this area that is still unknown. Anyway, I'm sure I'm boring you with all the Mesoamerican stuff, since I know that isn't your area.

Under the canopy of rainforest at the edge of El Lugar, we met an unrecorded tribe that calls itself Jio-Ontros, as near as we can phonetically record it. It seems they use an aspirant in some of their vowels that makes them hard to write in Roman letters. We conducted some initial research over the course of the week and have made amazing discoveries. I sent you the abstract for Dr. Hernández's report. I had Bucky translate it, so it should be pretty close.

Anyway, Dr. Hernández said that the most amazing part of the Jio-Ontros are the ruins that they venerate as sacred relics. We can't get to them because the tribe's big man refuses us entrance during their festival time, but from observations, it seems that we are dealing with a pre-classical Mayan-style city a thousand miles south of the Maya land.

When he found out that I called you about the Jio-Ontros, Dr. Hernández asked me to send you a cast of a small stone tablet for identification in the hope you'll come down here. He borrowed it from big man who apparently has a cache of extremely old ritual objects, and there are some that aren't broken.

***

DeQuin put the letter down without finishing it. He turned to the last page where Amanda had stapled a hand-written translation of the Hernández abstract, entitled "Description and Investigation into Jio-Ontros People of Costa Rica's Lugar de la Noche Negra." There was nothing of interest in the banalities of anthropology. However, the Greek on this almost unquestionably old artifact intrigued him. He picked up the telephone and called the anthropology department secretary.

"Patty," he said, "it's Mike DeQuin. I'm canceling my classes for the week. I have an important conference in San José that I completely forgot about.

Get my T.A. Ben to cover for me through Friday, would you?"

***

Prof. DeQuin arrived in Costa Rica early the next morning, having taken red-eye flights from Syracuse to JFK to San José. He had charged the plane tickets to his University account under the cover of a research "conference," figuring that the resulting sensation from the find would erase any impropriety in the school accountant's eyes. In truth, he was conferring, but not with a group of professors. There was only one man he wanted to talk with. He came to speak with Dr. Hernández. He hailed a cab and hurried out of the capital to the university in San Pedro.

Amanda, darker and thinner than DeQuin remembered her, was shocked to see her old professor in Costa Rica; in his haste he had forgotten to tell her he was coming. She took him immediately to Dr. Tomás Hernández, who, she warned, did not speak English. Amanda brought her boyfriend Bucky with her, and he acted as translator.

"Professor DeQuin, it is an honor to meet you," Hernández said. "You're expertise in matters archeo-anthropological is very important to me. Thank you for coming."

"You're welcome, doctor," DeQuin said. "Please tell me everything you know about the Jio-Ontros. How did you find them?"

"The local *rancheros* had told us that a drought had brought a strange people out from the woods toward the part of the river running across the *rancheros* pasture lands. They were not like other local *indios*, but were instead said to be *hombres blancos*, or white men like themselves."

"When did you first find these people?" DeQuin asked excitedly.

"On the ninth of March my team arrived in Lugar de la Noche Negra, an area encompassing several different areas of vegetation and a small river. It stands in the shadows of several mountains, and is the outer edge of the main Busca Roja rain forest, so named for the red color of the area's soil. We made contact later that day with a tribe which did not speak Spanish. Fortunately, one of our guides was from a local tribe whose language some of the Jio-Ontros knew through trade. Honestly, I found it hard to believe that any un-contacted tribes could survive into the twenty-first century.

"The people call themselves Jio-Ontros, but they do not know what the name means, only that it is different from an opposing group they call the Huestróntros. Of them they speak little save that they are an evil race that no Jio-Ontros deals with.

"The Jio-Ontros live in a small village of mud and wood huts. They are a hunter-gatherer people with a loose form of big man government. They possess many trinkets of exquisite workmanship which testify to their long-vanished glory. On the outside of their village lies the entrance to a city of stone, which seems based on a pre-Maya or maybe Olmec style, perhaps inspired by the cultures to the north. As you can guess, such a find is very exciting for me. Some satellite imagery had indicated an intriguingly geometric outline in the area ten years ago, but with limited resources, it wasn't our priority.

"Since they call it Huestróntrobolos or the City of the Huestróntros, it was considered taboo and off-limits to all but the highest shamans of the tribe, and of course distinguished visitors like myself. The big man told us that twice a year the shamans go to the City and perform age-old rituals of sacrifice to keep the Huestróntros from reclaiming the city before the end of the 'great cycle,' which appears to have a calendrical significance. As you know, the Maya believed their calendar would cycle to completion in 2012, and it is likely the Olmec and their yet unknown predecessors had some similar belief."

"Ah, the end of the world!" DeQuin said. "As I tell my students, that bit of rubbish is more contemporary invention than real mythology."

"In part," Hernández replied. "This is, in fact, the focus of my lifetime of research. The Maya themselves would have seen it as the end of the old cycle and the start of the new, like millenniums in the modern calendar. I'm sure, though, that it originally marked something of great importance related to the gods of creation, First Mother and First Father; but I think the Maya themselves probably only half-knew the original meaning of the date, derived, I think, from pre-Olmec sources that had different insights into the date's meaning. It is my theory that the pre-Olmec peoples, obsessed with astronomy, used the stars to mark a point in time when the great chaos monsters under the earth were supposed to arise, the creatures we know only through sculpture under modern names like the jaguar god and the rain god."

"Oh, yes, very similar to the Near Eastern beliefs about the upcoming reign of Satan or the release of the Zoroastrian chaos monster after the twelve thousand year cycle. Please, finish your story, I didn't mean to interrupt."

"You know your mythology, professor. There isn't much more. In exchange for the sacrifices, the Jio-Ontros said, the Huestróntros grant them whatever meager treasure they can cull from their crypts." At this point Hernández said there was no more to tell.

"But you say the people are whitish in color? Albinism?" DeQuin asked.

"I suppose that you could say they are white," Hernández said, "insofar as their skin sometimes appears lighter than the other native peoples of the area. However, there are no racial implications, since race is not a genetic thing, but is a response to climate. They live in the dark jungle and are correspondingly paler."

"But what of their language?"

"We were not able to classify their language, but a few words seem clearly to be borrowed from European tongues. We are organizing a full-scale expedition to study them in detail, but I don't believe that they are half as interesting as their city. That is what I want to explore in more detail, since I am an archaeologist after all. If it is truly an Olmec colony, it will be a great boon to our knowledge, for no Olmec city remains intact, and certainly nothing this far south of the Olmec heartland. If, as I believe, it is pre-Olmec, it would rewrite history."

"Dr. Hernández, I can only stay in Costa Rica a few days. Is there a chance that I could see this city before I return to America?"

"Well, our expedition would not leave until next season, since the wet season will be upon us any day now. However, if you would like, we could make an unofficial private tour tomorrow morning."

***

They left at dawn in a small plane that carried them to a grass-hewn air strip in the bland and formless village of Santa Maria de los Caballos. They disembarked and crossed the flat grassland to a pair of waiting Land Cruisers. They got inside the cars before the women of the village could attempt to sell them trinkets. DeQuin noticed that their drivers wore camouflaged fatigues and sat with a military stiffness.

"Who are the drivers?" DeQuin asked.

Hernández assured him that the drivers were off-duty soldiers making extra money as guides during the economic hardship of the highly unusual summer drought. They drove in virtual silence along dry dirt roads, kicking up clouds of dust into the hot and arid air. Under the blazing noon-time sun, they came to a parched section of brown grass sprawling before some wilted trees. Cows sheltered beneath the branches. The trees masked the green glory of the rainforest just over the hill.

Amanda leaned over to DeQuin and said, "We go on foot from here."

They walked with great effort up and over the hill. DeQuin, not used to the climate of Costa Rica, panted and drank too much water. As they approached the rain forest, Amanda thought to offer an exposition on the geologic formation of the area.

"You're standing on what used to be the beach. This whole plain was formed a couple thousand years ago when that mountain over there, San Cristóbol, erupted around 1000 B.C. or so. Before that, we think that the Jio-Ontros people were fishermen."

"Their city would have been on the coast, would it not?" DeQuin asked.

"We think it would have stood a mile or so inland, but that the river on your right would have connected the city with the ocean."

"That's not a river," DeQuin said.

"What do you mean?" Amanda asked.

"Look at it more carefully, Mandy. I noticed it when we flew over the area this morning. It's the only one like it in the region."

"Oh my God," Amanda said. "I didn't even notice. It's perfectly straight."

"That's right, straight until it hits the volcanism. It's not a river; it's a canal."

Amanda and Bucky quickly relayed the news to Dr. Hernández, who said something in Spanish.

"What did he say?" DeQuin asked.

"He says that he already knew but didn't want the secret out before he got his name on it in the journals."

They continued walking into the forest, where the atmosphere was much darker and moister than on the surrounding plane. Dr. Hernández signaled for them to stop, and he told them that they were approaching Jio-Ontros territory. They would detour around the tribe and approach the sacred city from the back. That way the tribe would not see them, since they visit the city but twice per year, and the jungle would cover them once inside the vine-encrusted city. This would avoid the social obligation to present the big man with yet more "gifts."

***

It did not take long for them to reach the city. It was only an hour's march from the edge of the forest, and they arrived with plenty of daylight left to explore its buildings. They planned to stay until the next afternoon, when they would return to their cars and drive back to the village a few miles away. Dr. Hernández pointed toward a tall stone structure, and the group headed toward it as the guides cut away the jungle before them.

"It's amazing," DeQuin said. "That temple must be seventy feet tall." He stared upward toward the masonry pyramid that itself looked upward past the meager rays of sun filtering through the forest canopy and through the roof formed of branches and leaves. Vines obscured the sculptures on its base, and a tree seemed to be growing from a hole in one side. Nevertheless, the edifice was astonishing in its grandeur, and it seemed incalculably old.

"What do the natives call this place again?" DeQuin asked.

"Their name for it is Huestróntrobolos," Amanda said. "They say that it means the City of the Huestróntros, but we don't know what that name means. According to the Jio-Ontros legends, this place was old even when they themselves arrived."

"The blocks they used are very large," DeQuin said. "If memory serves, these are about two or three times as large as the Mayan temple blocks up north in Guatemala."

"Dr. Hernández is of the opinion that Mayan temples were decadent imitations of something older, perhaps even predating the Olmec."

"Nonsense," DeQuin said. "Before the Olmec, there was nothing in the area."

"Nothing that we know of," Amanda corrected.

DeQuin cleared some vines from the wall and glanced at the sculptures carved on the pyramid's base. They were flamboyant mythological scenes of monstrous deities whose details had been effaced by centuries of pluvial erosion. Beside these figures, carved circles and lines seemed to record something, perhaps calendar dates in the fashion of the Olmec, whose only writing was a calendrical Morse code of dashes and dots later adopted by the Maya for their calculations. Beneath the panels of relief, he noticed some graffiti hastily carved. He looked at it twice before calling Amanda over.

"What does this look like?" he asked.

"It looks like hieroglyphs or writing of some kind."

"What kind of writing?"

"Well, if I had to guess, I'd say it resembled Linear B, but that's impossible."

"Why?"

"Well, there weren't any Greeks here, first of all."

"It's archaic Greek. I'm willing to bet on it."

"Well what does it say?" she asked.

"Hold on... It says, 'this is the place of the spawn of Tartarus.' It says something else I can't read . . . the letters are gone . . . and then 'I beg Zeus's aid.'"

"I can't believe it," Amanda said, "Greeks in America! This is going to make history! We're breaking new ground."

"Why didn't I think of it earlier?" DeQuin asked. "The names of the people here. The reason they don't sound Mayan or native is because they're Greek."

"What do you mean?"

"I'm pretty sure that the *ontros* in the Jio-Ontros's name refers to the Greek *anthros*, man. A few centuries of degradation and you end up with *ontros*."

"It would make sense because most tribes call themselves 'the humans' to differentiate from their enemies, whom they don't view as people."

"Professor! Mandy!" Bucky's voice called from the other side of the pyramid. "Dr. H. wants us to go up with him. Come on!"

The Americans and the Costa Rican archaeologist left their guides at the base of the building, and the four of them began to climb the front of the pyramid, up the uneven sacred steps that led toward a platform and temple atop the ritual mound. The climbing was slow, and the progress hard. The steps were gigantic in size, as though made for beings twice as tall as man, so each level was a struggle to ascend. As they grunted and huffed their way up, DeQuin kept turning over the mystery in his mind.

"What does it mean?" he kept thinking. "Jio-Onthros. Jio-Anthros. Jio-. . ."

"Professor!" Bucky called. "What do you make of the pyramid's geometry? It seems off somehow."

"That's it!" DeQuin shouted. "Jio-Onthros is *Geo-Anthros*... Earth-Men!"

"Sssshhhh!" Amanda cautioned. "Don't let Dr. Hernández hear you. This could make my career. I don't want him getting all the credit."

"Hernández has all the credit he needs with finding this place; the linguistic stuff is going to be our little project. Greeks in America! Think of it! *The Odyssey* as fact."

"That's great, Professor DeQuin, but what does the other name mean?"

"What name?"

"Huestróntros"

"Well, let's see... If we assume it's Greek like the other name, then *ontros* means 'man' once again. So we have *huestro-anthros*. Hmmm.... If *huestro* is Hernández's Spanish corruption of the original we could have *ostro* maybe."

"That's it," Amanda said. "The natives said either *ostro* or *ah-stro*. The spelling was Hernández's Spanish transliteration."

"Then we have *astro-anthros*. . . Star-Men?. . . Interesting."

"Then this place is *astro-anthro-bolos*. What's *bolos*?" Amanda asked.

"Not *bolos*. I think it's a corruption of *polis*. *Astroanthropolis*. Star-Man City. An observatory perhaps?"

By now they had all but reached the top of the pyramid, and the little party stopped to gaze out over the city spread before them. From pockets of foliage, they could see the roofs and towers of long-abandoned masonry and what seemed to be colossal stone heads poking from clumps of ferns. Trees cut through ancient walls, and fallen stones lay all about the low-rising ground cover.

Prof. DeQuin noticed that the buildings seemed built on an unfamiliar geometric grid. Something was not quite right. He wondered if an earthquake had disturbed the city in ages past. How else to account for the strange and unique angles the foundations traced in the soft ground.

"*Aquí es Huestróntrobolos!*" triumphantly exclaimed Dr. Hernández. "*Vengan ustedes conmigo.*"

"What did he say?" DeQuin asked.

"He said to come with him," Bucky replied.

They all followed Dr. Hernández inside the dark, narrow door of the chamber atop the pyramid. They glanced around the square chamber built within a cube of masonry outlined in wide, squat pillars, like a miniature Greek temple flattened by a giant's step. The interior was unlit, and DeQuin rummaged his backpack for his flashlight. He flicked it on, as the others did with their instruments, and they looked at walls stripped bare of all ornamentation through countless centuries of neglect. Occasionally the remains of a relief or carving hinted at tentacled deities not uncommon for maritime peoples to worship in their esoteric and occult rites, but no image was clear enough to identify precisely what it was that the artists wished to depict.

DeQuin had the feeling that these carvings were infinitely older than the decadent Greeks who must have stumbled upon them when some cruel twist of chance led them to this dark city. The building felt too *old*, too primeval to have been a Greek invention, for were the Greeks not masters of light and joyous architecture? This then must have been the style of construction that the later Maya would turn into their great temples, the very archetype from which classic New World civilization would grow. And to think that he, Michael T. DeQuin, professor of anthropology at Marius University, was among the first to see this great temple.

"As you can see, Professor," Dr. Hernández said, "this is a very special place. If you look around, you can see carved into the walls the remains of columns of dots and dashes. These are calendrical markers—the earliest known in all Mesoamerica. I believe they read the same way that Olmec and Mayan calendars do, and—this is of course a guess pending more research—they appear to indicate something like the Maya Long Count but carved all the way back at the beginning—the very time when the calendar began. That small carving there, in the corner, is, I believe, the end of the count with a strange image, half-effaced, of some demon or god emerging. It is all very exciting."

DeQuin swung the flashlight around to search the floor for artifacts lest he inadvertently step on something important as he made his way toward the spot on the wall Hernández had indicated. He noticed then that the center of this chamber held a pentagonal and very deep black hole.

"Watch out!" he shouted to Bucky, who had taken a step toward the middle of the room without first checking the floor.

"What?" Bucky called as he tripped on the edge and fell forward, his leg catching in the hole as he tumbled over onto the floor.

"Oh my God! Bucky!" Amanda shrieked, and both she and DeQuin lurched forward to help Bucky, who had injured his ankle in his fall.

DeQuin shined his flashlight downward, but the beam vanished into the vastness of the hole, only in one place seeming to momentarily reflect off something shiny and pulsing, though this might have been an illusion. They smelled a tremendous odor from whatever moved at the bottom of the temple, a stench so inhuman that it sickened DeQuin and burned his nostrils and throat. A rumbling noise came and went, like a heavy object being dragged across a field of broken glass. Then, the smell subsided.

The Costa Rican professor indicated to Bucky and to Amanda that he wanted them to translate for DeQuin. Bucky groaned in pain, and Amanda began the translation.

"The Maya," he said, "they did not know so much about the calendar or the temples. They adapted and adopted what they found here, and in the other cities like this one, the ones that are down under the sea now after the oceans rose. The Olmec, they were closer in time to the people of this city, so they might have known more. The words, as they say, but not the music."

"What's going on here?" Amanda asked.

"The thing down under the temple, it is sleeping now. I was not quite sure at first, which is why Professor DeQuin was so valuable. It did not occur to me that the Jio-Ontros were Greek, and that solves a bit more of the puzzle. I can see now that they were just chance visitors, maybe blown here by accident. They did not build the city. The star-men did, the ones that live down under this city and under the others."

"What others?" DeQuin asked.

"Oh, surely you know of the others. There is one near Cuba, one at Bimini, and another at Yonaguni off the coast of Japan. The underwater stone cities thousands of years older than human civilization. I have never been to Ponape, but there is supposed to be one in the sea beneath Nan Madol. They are the ancient seats of the beings that came from the stars. They are asleep, but they set the alarm, told us when they would wake up. The calendar you see around you, the one the Maya so carefully preserved for who knows how many centuries, is not simply a marker of the end of the world. It is, I believe, a cosmic alarm clock."

"This is ridiculous," DeQuin said.

"Is it? You yourself called them star men, and you glimpsed what is down there. Can you doubt that this temple, with its fabulous workmanship, and the city in all its splendor are something more than the work of jungle tribes? Why the coincidence in sites and myths around the world? You discussed them yourself--end of the world stories the world over. I spent my whole life waiting to find something like this, and I have no doubt that this is the citadel of beings that came, as the Mayan myths say, from the sky at the creation of the world."

"I simply cannot accept that some five thousand year old alien is blubbering under this temple and scrawled on the walls a 'do not disturb until X-mas 2012' sign."

"Then you and I differ. You do not have faith in things unseen. But I for one will be here that day, watching and waiting for the glorious resurrection."

"You're mad, Hernandez. This is all madness."

"Is it? What did your Greeks see that made them stay here for three thousand years guarding this temple and making sacrifices in this pit? What did the Olmec tell them about this place? Can you really say you don't want to know?"

"There is simply no proof..."

"The fact, professor, are the facts whether you like them or not. Yes, I admit there is speculation here, but can you tell me that you will ever again look at an ancient temple and not wonder just what it is really commemorating? Are you saying that when the calendar runs out soon, you won't pause just for a minute to wonder what shakes the earth and lights the sky?"

The Costa Rican paused and gazed longingly into the pit. A blast of foul air wafted up from the pit amidst a guttural rumbling.

"I spent my whole life," he resumed quietly, "studying Mayan and Olmec culture, especially their calendars and mythology. But the things I have seen here, they changed everything. I am asking you, professor, who know of pre-classical Greeks as I do Olmec, to help me work with the Jio-Ontros and learn everything there is to know about this place before it is too late. Stay here, and be witness to the greatest discovery in all history. Surely, like any scientist, you must have a hunger to know the truth."

Professor DeQuin stood silently in the temple and gazed out the narrow door, letting his eyes fall on the unstable angles of the city's unique architecture, visible only dimly and in part through the canopy of trees. To explore an alien landscape would be, in its way, the culmination of any anthropologist's life's work and the academic immortality he sought as well. But, too, there was the thing in the pit, which he hoped was nothing more than geologic gases like those that sparked the myth of Python and the oracle of Apollo's temple at Delphi. But he had seen and smelled--or had he?--the thing that rolled and moved beneath the stones, and too the calendar on the temple walls ended in a carving of some creature rising up from the depths. If on some small chance--clearly impossible--the Maya were right, was this where he wished to see through the end?

DeQuin breathed deeply of the cool breeze blowing through the outer door. He turned and gazed down into the abyss, waited for the half-seen thing to reappear. As the noise and smell returned, he shined his light downward more purposefully and strained his eyes to fathom what moved beneath him. And he made his decision.

***

Two years later and a few pounds heavier, Professor DeQuin celebrated the end of another semester and the upcoming Christmas holiday with his usual bottle of fine wine and a night spent on his sofa watching DVDs of his favorite old British sitcoms. It did not entirely surprise him when the dark, star-spangled night sky began to glow bright, and he shut the curtains to block out the unnatural light. Elsewhere, in a warmer part of the world, crowds stampeded and screamed, and the earth shook with the titan force of *something* DeQuin had once seen and did not care to see again.

He turned up the volume on his television and poured another glass of wine. He had a feeling that this might well be a very long night indeed.

Against the Storm

By Trent Roman

Two flickering sources of light drew the huddled students to inevitably congregate around them. The first, most obvious, was the bonfire that smoked up to the hole practiced into the granite of the temple ceiling, as it surely had in ancient times, though it was possibly the first time the carved emblems along the wall and ceiling had felt the charry caress of soot again after centuries of being forgotten. Ordinarily, those now stoking the embers would be the first to express their dismay at the potential damage the smoke was inflicting on the irreplaceable ruins—but greater horrors than this occupied their thoughts this night.

The second light source was significantly less bucolic in nature, but, in the long run, probably less useful than the fire. Already the pale blue glow of the portable's screen flickered and even cut out to a blank readout as the irradiated ionosphere scrambled the signal, earth-bound humanity continued trying to relay to the satellites safely in orbit. And that wasn't counting the fact that the global thunderstorm which had shrouded most of the planet had, by now, certainly caused a fair amount of damage to the physical infrastructure that sustained the informational aether, condemning whole swathes of the species to suffer in silence.

There was something perverse about watching the world come to an end in intermittent updates; it was a futile vigil, but many of those gathered here, Levy included, couldn't help but hang on every tidbit that struggled through the collapsing network, rubbernecking across international boundaries and continents. Lizbeth Morris wished she could be sitting with those by the fire, companionable in their silent defeatism, but the glimmers of the wider world that she could still intercept on her handheld felt like the closest she could get to the comfort of familiarity. What she really wanted right now was the harsh Nebraska homestead of her youth (long since sold to developers), the sustenance of family, and the boyfriend who was still States-side. In this anachronistic fantasy, she was being held, body to body, the immediate physical sense a blanket that warded away fear the way a beloved doll kept the bedroom monsters at bay; nothing could truly provide shelter against the terrible fury of the sky, but where impotence held sway illusion became the most valuable thing.

As though to remind her of the reality of their situation, a sequence of lightning bolts crackled across the ebon sky, momentarily making the ruins of Site K as well lit as if it were midday, albeit with diffuse light rather than the directed white-yellow of the treasonous sun. The lightning never truly stopped, of course—not with the planet's radiation-suffused atmosphere—but it was a testament to how a person could adapt to any ambient condition that she no longer noticed it, or the constant thunder, nor the driving rain and hail, unless there was a particularly terrible burst that stood out against the white noise of apocalypse.

"Hawaii," Lizbeth said after a new burst of static interference was past, her tone exactly what you'd expect of a person reading a casualty list that wouldn't end: flat, hollow... Yet, there was an undercurrent of the same rabid, jabbering panic that Levy sensed lurking around the back of her mind, the all-devouring black panther in the neuron jungle.

"What are they saying?" someone in the circle asked.

Lizbeth shrugged. "The same. An unbroken horizon of thunderstorms. Lightning. It's already begun to hail." She paused. "They say the ocean swell is rising."

"Is this going to cause tidal waves, you think?"

This from Clark 'Kent' Comiskey, who, unlike Levy, was a veteran of Site K. His thesis, if Levy remembered correctly, was a study of the trade links between the classical Maya and the various island chiefdoms in the Caribbean. They were on the wrong side of Mexico for that right now—the Pacific Ocean was just on the other side of the Sierra Madre mountain range—but students took what digs they could get, as close to their specialty as could be managed.

Lizbeth Morris, for her part, was a paleoclimatologist—always handy to have on Mayan digs, given the varied and contentious theories putting forward ecological causes for the civilization's collapse—and was, at the moment, the closest thing they had to an expert on the unfurling disaster.

"Tidal waves? No, not in the technical sense. But storm surge, yes, and given that this is the biggest storm since... since the last time this happened... the flooding is bad enough to cover a lot of low-lying inland areas as well as the coasts. Like with the Netherlands..."

She drifted off. The storm had formed over East Asia, but the downpour hadn't begun until Europe and Africa were in line to get the worst of the radiation pouring from the giant solar flares roiling across the surface of the sun. Levy imagined that all that solar radiation would have deleterious effects in the long term—cancer, crop failures and all that—but little could compare to the immediate devastation caused by that radiation supercharging the ionosphere with electricity, a surplus that could only be a series of disastrous storm cells that had grown until all affected parts of the globe were covered under a seemingly unbroken veil of thunderheads.

The lightning, the wind, the hail all pounded the earth and caused havoc where they landed, but it was the water that would cause the greatest damage, oceans besieging shorelines and overflowing rivers gouging the land. The last news to come out of Europe had indicated flooding on an unprecedented scale, and Levy didn't doubt the American Midwest would soon follow; the remnants of her childhood drowned under several feet of the gluttonous Missouri River. Then, in a few hours, as the world's rotation finished quilting the planet's shroud from the persistent radiation, China and the rest of Asia would face the floods.

"We just need to sit put; we'll be fine," Professor Terrell said, filling the lull with what had become, for him, a mantra. To Levy, the bearded, middle-aged man seemed to have shrunk since the day before, to have somehow lost tangible presence. She used to look up to him as proof that it was possible to make a career out of what she loved against the protestations of family and friends that her vocation was too esoteric; plus, as a likely supervisor, he was imbued with authority no matter how friendly he tried to be with his students. Now, though, there was only a fellow refugee, and no future to be embodied. They still deferred to him out of habit or shellshock, but there was no power there—it was merely a default condition, easily overturned.

And, as though to confirm her thoughts, she heard a sound of derision from the circle around the fire. That one was about half students, half locals—bodyguards hired in Tapachula, on the off chance that they ran into what few jaguars still roamed this jungle, or Zapatistas agitated by the latest government crackdown. The expedition had also been accompanied by a number of native guides from nearby villages, themselves descendants of the Maya, but they had left when the scope of the storm had become apparent, to ride out Armageddon with their families back home, something Levy envied greatly.

But it was one of the students who had made the noise; he rose now, ambled the short distance between the two clusters, and Levy, squinting against the light of the fire, and was able to make out the scrawny, fashionably unshaven features of Shane Oliver. The PhD candidate was an expert in Maya religion, mythology and iconographic, whose facility at reading the claustrophobically tight hieroglyphic script of the carved cartouches in the ruins had impressed her greatly. As he stood at the edge of the screen's glow, however, Levy thought there was something about his countenance, something about the way he kept shifting his weight from foot to foot and how his eyes roved apparently without goal, which made her anxious.

"We'll be fine?" he echoed. "It's the day of reckoning. We've been judged and found wanting, and we can expect no mercy from the gods for what we've done."

A few people glanced desultorily in his direction.

"Think about it!" Oliver said, half-crouching, hands curled into claws. "The only people who knew—the only ones who could have warned us—and what did we do? We killed and raped and plundered, burned their knowledge, practiced genocide on their culture and left them to die slowly of poverty and marginalization while we come here to strip away the very last vestiges of their civilization and bring it home with us and pat ourselves on the back for it because we're so much smarter and we can appreciate the history—the *history*! Well, we're appreciating it now, aren't we? Front row seats to history fulfilled and our own destruction!"

"Calm down, Shane," Professor Terrell said, waving an open palm in a placating gesture. "The storm will pass—it did before. We just need to ride it out and hope to avoid the worst of it. This temple is good shelter, solid stonework; it's stood the test of centuries—"

"Centuries?" Oliver scoffed. "What do centuries matter when we're talking about the ages of the world?" He threw his hands into the air, unintentionally but no less dramatically backlit by the flickering firelight, and Levy thought that all he needed now was a ritual mask to look like a shaman out of ages past. "We lived in the Fourth World, which will be destroyed on the winter solstice, 2012 as our calendar reckons it, to usher in the Fifth. So it was written and so it has come to pass! Even you can't deny that this day has been long predicted; the gods of thunder and lightning will not spare us for our ignorance."

"No one's denying anything," Terrell said, shaking his head, "But let's not lose our objectivity. This isn't a mystical event;" he waved towards Lizbeth Morris, "Climatic sciences know and understand why this is happening. It's obvious that this, ah, solar flare activity... thing... is a cyclical event, occurring every few thousand years, and that the Maya—or more likely, a predecessor civilization—were able to note, remember and calculate the next occurrence of the cycle. A unique achievement, to be sure, but that doesn't mean anything for the associated mythology."

"Cyclical global storms—and the flooding we're seeing now—probably account for the prevalence of flood myths worldwide," Levy put in. "Another form of cultural remembrance."

"Yes, thank you, Gina," Terrell said, falling back into pedagogical tone, albeit one empty of his usual enthusiasm for his subject. "And I think such stories can also help us put our current situation into context: this isn't the end of the world. Humanity has survived one and probably several such events in the past, and that was with the most basic technology and a mere fraction of the current global population. We'll endure, we'll rebuild, and this time we'll make sure that future generations will remember what's coming so they can figure out how to stop it or adapt to it."

"See that?" Oliver said, pacing. "That's *exactly* the kind of hubris that led us into this situation. The idea that *we* can dictate to nature and defy what is clearly divine will. Wrong-headed belief, false comfort, just like the idea that these walls will protect us from the heavens asunder. These are ruins—they couldn't even keep disuse and the jungle at bay, let alone the wrath of Chaac, the lightning god."

"The Long Count in buildings of this area are older than any other, go back further—" Comiskey began, but Oliver jumped in.

"And? Even the oldest stella barely tracks a few decades before the common era."

Levy was forced to admit that Oliver was correct: the Mayans' calendar went back millennia—by comparison, even these ancient ruins were recent.

"What would you suggest then, Shane?" Terrell said, rising his arms in interrogation, his voice tired. "Where could we go?"

Oliver hesitated, and then began to wave his finger. "The stories—the stories will be our guide. Chaac is the lightning god, yes?" Before anybody could agree, Oliver ploughed on: "How was the lightning god defeated the last time. By the maize god! It was him—or her—who negotiated the truce last time; we have to summon him so he can save humanity again. Yes, yes—that's what we have to do."

"Summon a god?" Lizbeth shook her head. "Listen to yourself, man. You're losing it."

"Shut up," he hissed, and Morris recoiled from the hostility in his voice. Levy was taken aback, too; she wouldn't have thought the typically aloof doctoral candidate could condense such contempt in two little words. "I'm thinking here," he added, drumming his fingers along his jaw line. "Palenque."

"Palenque?" Levy echoed, frowning. Everybody knew about Palenque—it was the most famous Mayan temple complex in the area, with such incredible artwork that it made Site K look like a shack. But she couldn't see what it had to do with their situation.

"Yes, Palenque—it has a temple devoted to the maize god. That's where we need to go if we want to be safe from Chaac; where we'll be able to awaken the maize god and save the world!"

"Shane, you're not well—you're not thinking straight. The stress..." Professor Terrell said. "We can't go to Palenque; it's clear on the other side of the state. There's jungle, there's the Sierra Norte range; it would be several days' hiking, even if conditions were good which, if you haven't noticed, they aren't."

"Fine," Oliver sneered. "Stay here and die. I'm going to Palenque."

With that, he turned abruptly on his heels and stalked out of the stone ruins, not breaking his stride at all as he hit the sheets of rain and hail beating the jungle beyond. Levy watched, incredulous, as he pushed his way past foliage and disappeared into the darkness of the storm.

"Well?" she asked, turning back to look at the rest of the group. "Isn't anybody going to stop him?"

"What the hell for?" Lizbeth groused. "He's out of his mind."

"Obviously—and that's why we should stop him! He's going to get himself killed out there, wandering the jungle in this storm." Her statement met with echoing apathy. "That's it? No-one cares that we've let a colleague suffering a mental breakdown wander away to certain death?"

"What should we have done, Gina?" Professor Terrell asked. "Sat on him? Knocked him out with a rock?"

"If it works, yes! We should go after him, bring him back."

"It's too dangerous out there," Terrell said. "Anybody who goes looking for him is just as likely to get hurt themselves."

"Nobody should die alone," she said. "Besides he can't have gotten that far." She paused, waited to see if anybody was going to react, but they all looked back at her with glum expressions. "Great," she said, turning around, grabbing a yellow rain poncho from the pile. "Nice to see solidarity in times of crisis."

"Ah, the hell with it," Clark Comiskey said, rising from his stone. "I'll come with you."

Levy smiled back at the sturdy student. She knew he was a committed bodybuilder—his sculpted physique had earned him the nickname 'Kent', after the superhero, and being otherwise unattached, was frequently involved in the serial liaisons that gathered over the course of a dig as surely as artifacts and data. Even if Oliver got violent, Levy was sure Comiskey could handle him.

She waited another few seconds to see if Comiskey's act of camaraderie had stirred anybody else to the endeavor, but their fellows only looked back at them with haunted, tired expressions. Shrugging, Levy turned back to the jungle and strode forward into the darkness.

She regretted her decision almost as soon as she stepped out of the relative protection of the ruins, as her poncho was beaten on by rain and small bits of hail. The cold wind had all given them all chills before—it was one of the reasons they had built the fire, the other being for some light amid the darkness of the storm—but now, combined with the rain, it felt as though this sub-tropical rainforest had just turned into a springtime slog through a wintry, boreal forest. Except at least then the ground would be solid, rather than the endless mud that squelched beneath her dig boots, sucking at her every step. While the poncho kept her head and shoulders fairly dry, the rest of her clothes were soaked through within the space of a minute, the wind forcing them against her like a second skin of cold wetness.

She almost turned back, almost admitted defeat just for the relative warmth and shelter of the ruins. She thought she could stand the knowing stares, the blow to her pride, the silent acknowledgement that she couldn't hold herself to the standards she had challenged the others to uphold. What she couldn't stand was the idea of someone she knew lying, bleeding and alone, on some godforsaken patch of storm-wracked jungle, facing a certain end without so much as the presence of a relative stranger to help ease the passing. It was that image that kept her going, forging a path through the brush as Comiskey followed behind, although she wouldn't admit to it, it wasn't Oliver face she saw in her mind's eye, bloodied and tear-streaked, when lightning lit the jungle, but her own.

"Shane!" she screamed into the wind, against a mouthful of tasteless rain. "Oliver Shane! Come on, man, where are you?"

Comiskey took up the call; his voice was louder and carried further than hers, but still there was no response.

"Are you sure he went this way?" Comiskey asked.

"I think so," Levy screamed back, although she was increasingly uncertain of that. When they had set off she had been able to follow a broken path of underbrush through the jungle, but with the darkness making it hard to see, and the wind whipping the jungle into new patterns at every moment, now she only thought that they were heading in the general direction in which Oliver had gone. And that was assuming he hadn't gone off in another direction, which was entirely possible—he had fixated on Palenque, and that meant north, but Levy wasn't sure how far one could trust in the consistency of someone who had so clearly gone off the deep end like Oliver had.

The pair of them pushed forward, one mud-caked boot in front of the other, further dragged down by clothes that felt as heavy as if she were trying to swim fully dressed. Levy began to feel as though she'd be better off just getting rid of them altogether, to stave off the cold and restore some mobility, but then the wind would whip branches from her hands and slash leaves across her face, and she would be grateful for the protection they offered. She was breathing heavily now, straining from the exertion of pushing against wind, foliage and mud; archaeology was a physical pursuit and kept one trim as surely as any exercise routine, but under these conditions merely walking was exhausting. Her only comfort was that Comiskey, when she turned back to look at him, looked just as winded as she did, his face red and muscles taut beneath an T-shirt that had turned translucent from the pounding rain.

"I think we're going uphill," he shouted at her.

"Are we?" Levy looked around, trying to orientate herself. It wasn't easy; this jungle might have been endangered, beset by deforestation and other forms of human encroachment, but at its heart it was as thick as any rainforest, and gave little in way of line of sight. She spotted a large, flat rock and clambered onto it, searching the canopy. Comiskey was right: while her vision was blocked in most directions, the way they had come she could see a lot more of the jungle, including the top of the trees. Including...

"I can see the top of the temple from here," she called down to Comiskey.

"Maybe we should go back?" he suggested.

Seeing the distant shelter, Levy felt her resolve waver. She didn't really want to get so far out that they wouldn't be able to make their way back, after all. She could say that she gave it her best try, that at least she hadn't accepted the loss without doing anything.

Then she heard a voice carried on the wind; she couldn't make out the words (assuming there were any and it wasn't a random assortment of gibbering), but it was definitely a man, and one screaming rather loudly.

"Oliver?" she asked Comiskey.

"Can't imagine anybody else crazy enough to be out here," he answered.

Except us, Levy thought, but didn't say it aloud. She turned until she thought she had a good angle on the sound—the wind and the strange sound tunnels created by the heavy plant life made such estimations difficult—and the two of them set out with renewed purpose.

It quickly became evident that Oliver was climbing the hilly escarpment, heading for higher ground—not a bad instinct, in Levy's opinion, except that it made catching up to him all the more arduous. Site K (so named for the large carving of the unnamed Mayan God K at the entrance) was located in a highland valley, but there were mountain ranges to both sides, and smaller hills such as these dotted the valley. As they climbed, the vegetation became sparser, more scraggly. This was a mixed blessing at best—Levy could hardly believe it, but the rain and hail was even worse now, without the canopy to deflect the precipitation.

"This is getting really dangerous," Comiskey called at her, holding his poncho taut over his head to act as a shield against the hail.

As though in response, they heard another round of screams coming from above—Oliver, sounding more and more as though his psychotic break was deepening.

"We're almost there, come on," Levy said, arranging her poncho the same way. With their arms occupied, it became even more of a challenge to keep their balance, although at least the ground here was more solid, with a number of stones that could be used as a kind of improvised staircase.

Levy didn't notice the noise at first, hidden in the white noise of thunder, but eventually the rumbling became impossible to deny. They paused to look around, and finally Comiskey seized her shoulder and pointed her to the southeast. It seemed as though a large swathe of the rainforest had suddenly become mobile, running down the side of the hill like ice cream melting in the sun, carving a discolored gouge in the jungle where it passed, a grayish-brown patch of packed earth and debris.

It was a landslide, Levy recognized instantly, although she didn't know why she ought to be surprised: all this rain was no doubt weakening the soil even as the hail beat away at the trees, making it terribly likely that the slope would just collapse in an avalanche of loose earth. Levy worried whether the same thing might happen on the slope they were on now—if the hill let go, there would be no way to outrun or escape such a cascade. Maybe it would be better to just head back to the temple and—

"Oh my god, the temple!" Levy cried out, suddenly realizing that what she had took to be a large swathe of stone in the debris field was in fact the top of the ruins at Site K—the landslide had engulfed the remnants of the old Mayan temple, burying it beneath meters of roiling soil... and everybody who had been inside...

"We have to go back," Levy cried, refusing to acknowledge what she knew: there would be no way to get to the ruins and dig out anybody before they die of asphyxia, even if they had survived the initial impact. "Clark, we have to—Clark?"

Levy looked around and found her partner lying on the ground a short distance away, body being beaten by the rain and hail without him so much as turning to avoid the blows. She bent down next to him, screaming his name; she turned his head to face her, and saw a great red gouge running from the corner of his eye to his temple, damage she could only imagine had been inflicted by a particularly large or serrated chunk of hail. He was still alive, but his eyes rolled about, unfocused, and his breathing was irregular as she pressed him to her, trying to find some way to staunch the flood of blood mixing with the rainwater down his cheek and across their clothes. His jaw worked, lips moved, but no sound came out of it; Levy thought he was concussed, but had no idea what she was going to do about it, trapped in the jungle, beset by the storm, with the rest of her team buried along with the only shelter she knew of.

Somewhere further up she heard a cawing that turning into wild, insane laughter; Oliver, sounding more like kind of demented animal than a person. She didn't know if he had seen the landslide or understood what it meant, but from the sound of it, she thought what little had been left of his sanity had finally broken under the assault of the elements, and he had given himself over to the storm, his mind reflecting the chaos outside. She wrote him off, mentally dismissing him: another loss.

Cradling Comiskey's feverishly warm body to her, Levy crawled back, trying in vain to find some sort of shelter from the perpetual hail. As another barrage of lightning lit up the wounded rainforest and the sickly brown patch of the landslide, Levy realized that it had all been in vain, not that she had much of a chance to begin with. It looked like she was going to die alone after all.

THE CANTICLE OF CHAK CHEL

By David A. Hewitt

The Mayan calendar's 5,126-year Long Count will reach its end on the winter solstice of the year 2012. Some hold that this presages the end of a World Age -- our era of scientific materialism -- and a return to the spiritual values of the ancients.

It's beginning again, in the chamber above.

The others are all gone now, taken away one by one; you are the last. The room is dark. The lamps that once lit up the world at night are gone now. The door is barred from the outside. Its wood is hard; it doesn't chip.

The Canticle begins with the chorus, with all the voices spilling together into one. You cover your ears, but you've heard this too many times; the words echo in the room above

*but they echo in your mind, too, and clamping your hands,
clamping your forearms against your ears doesn't silence
them...*

***

Chak Chel, sacred Mother
Chak Chel, who brings life
Her hand rules the rivers and all-drinking Sea
Chak Chel watches over each new-born, each child
Every new life that draws breath on this Earth

***

*You sit upright on your sleeping-pallet, wide awake. A
woman's voice begins the chant, flowing, beautiful:*

Always there was the Sea beneath the Sky. The
Sea eternal. The Sea that breathes with wind and
moon. And in the Sea was life -- voiceless life, it did
not praise its Makers. It sang no word of praise to the
Gods.

And the Gods spoke the name Earth and from
the Sea it arose: land rose from the Sea as a great turtle
breaks the surface of a lake, rivulets streaming from its
many-peaked shell. In the land was life, and the Gods
heard the voice of life, but this voice was chaos --
chattering, grunting, screeching chaos that did not
honor its Makers.

To the land came Chak Chel -- her hips broad,
her will as relentless as waves beating against the
shore, and she bore in her arms a great clay vessel
graven with many forms. Chak Chel wandered the
land. She saw the rivers and the lakes, and the beasts
that drank of their waters.

Then Chak Chel went to the gathering-place of
the Gods, a sward of rich green amidst cloud-haunted
heights, and She said to the Gods:

"The beasts are abundant, they thrive on the land. But as I walked the land they did not know me. Let us make one final creature, most helpless of all and naked as clay, one who will worship and sacrifice to the Gods."

Other Gods had walked, or soared over the land, and they agreed: the beasts, the trees, the waters, the stones -- these did not know their Makers. So Chak Chel's counsel ruled the day. This final creation was man, and Chak Chel watched over his birth. She bathed him in waters from the broad rim of her graven vessel and man was thankful; he swore he would repay the Gods for this gift of life.

***

All sing:
Chak Chel, sacred Mother
Chak Chel, who gives life
Her wisdom guides waters ever called to the Sea
Chak Chel watches over each new-born, each child
Every new life that draws breath on this Earth

***

A man's voice, deep, confident:
So humans dwelt in the land, our grandfathers and grandmothers worshipped the Gods, they feared the Gods, and it went well. The land was rich, and in the land were beasts. But the beasts fled like the unseen wind between leaves and through grass; they would not become man's food. The trees sheltered them. The ground hid them. And other beasts hunted man, for he was slow of foot, and his flesh tender.

Then to the Gods of the beasts, to their hidden home in the jungle's sunless heart, came Chak Chel, strong in her youth, face fierce and eyes wide. To the Gods of the beasts She said:

"Look upon man. See his need. Feed him in his hunger; protect him in his weakness."

But Rabbit-God, hiding in the arms of his mother the Moon, said:

"My children will flee from man. My sons and daughters will eat the Earth's fruits, hidden from the eye and safe from the hand of man."

Jaguar-God had long watched man, yellow eyes smoldering, jagged mouth slavering, and He said:

"My sons and daughters will feed on man. They will bedeck their jungle with the bones and blood of man's children."

But Chak Chel spoke again:

"The rabbit is indeed clever and none can match the jaguar's stealth, her grace. But clever as he is, the rabbit does not know his Maker; and though the jaguar's cry is like a thunderclap, she raises no song of praise to the Gods. Humans have wisdom. Protect them; teach them the ways of the beasts. They will praise you and sacrifice to you the rich blood of the hunt, for humans alone fear the Gods."

***

You rise in the dark, you ram the door with your shoulder, but it's solid, solid as the walls.

An old man's voice from above, trembling with piety:

So the Gods taught humans the ways of the beasts, and our grandfathers and grandmothers worshipped the Gods; they feared the Gods of the jungle and the Gods of the beasts, and it went well. Chak Chel guarded over every birth as man's numbers grew: his children were many, they flourished under

Sun and Sky like a river drinking the summer rains.
But still they wandered as beasts do in search of food;
they lived as beasts live.

Then Chak Chel, her head wrapped in twisted
cloth colored like the rainbow, came to Maize-God's
sun-dappled palace. Chak Chel spoke to Maize-God:

"Honored Maize-God, look upon man. See his
need. He lives in the land, he sings the praises of the
Gods, yet still he lives as the beasts live. Grant man
mastery over his hunger. Teach him the secrets of
planting. Man's mind knows the Gods. Man's heart
loves the Gods. Must men live as the groaning beasts
live?"

And Maize-God, tall Maize-God, leaned gently
toward Chak Chel, his crest of silken hair like a
fountain above her, and He whispered:

"The maize is my beloved child; it obeys only
me. I call it forth from the ground, I clothe it in many
colors; and when its day is ended, I lay it to sleep in a
soft bed of the richest soil."

Then Chak Chel said:

"Maize-God, teach humans the secrets of
maize. Teach them and they will guard the maize, they
will till the soil and maize will prosper. It will grow in
many fields in great abundance and humans will
dampen those fields with the blood of sacrifice, to feed
and honor the God whose maize nourishes their own
children."

***

All sing:
Chak Chel, sacred Mother
Chak Chel, who gives life
Great Keeper of lakes and streams born of the Sea
Chak Chel watches over each new-born, each child

Every new life that draws breath on this Earth
***

An old woman's voice, gruff, experienced:

So man mastered the maize and humankind lived like beasts no longer. Indeed, they mastered the beasts and the beasts served them. With Chak Chel watching over every woman's birth throes, man's numbers grew. Our grandfathers and grandmothers sacrificed to the Gods of the plants and to the Gods of the beasts, and it went well.

Then Chak Chel, her breasts weary from nourishing the needs of man's children came to Itzamna, Greatest of All, who sat on the band of the Sky and watched over its turning. To Itzamna She spoke:

"Honored Itzamna, Greatest of All, look upon man. Man worships the Gods, he praises the Gods. Teach him your secrets. Teach him the stars in their seasons that he might venture across Earth and Sea and return again to his own place."

Itzamna, First Giver of Names, turned to her. His wispy white hair streamed through the air above his flowered head-band, and his eyes were the Sun burning down on Chak Chel.

"The stars are mine. They keep the very truth of Creation and humankind shall never know their secrets. The stars will be ever out of reach, a reminder to man that he is small, a clod upon the Earth and nothing more."

But Chak Chel, pillared on stout legs, set her feet and met the eyes of Itzamna, and She said:

"Have pity on humans. They are small and Earth and Sea are wide. The stars of the Sky are as the glittering waves of the Sea, beyond counting. But teach man the secrets of the night Sky. Teach him and he will make even the stars tell tales of the might and the splendor of the Gods. For even the stars, their numbers beyond count, their radiance undying, give no thanks to the Gods who made them so. Humans alone offer praise, offer rich, flowing blood as sacrifice to the Gods who made Earth, Sea, and Sky."

***

So humans mapped the distant stars, and the stars silently guided man as he walked the wide Earth, and as he sailed the encircling Sea. Chak Chel stood ever beside the children of men as they scattered across the Earth and took root where they came to rest, like seeds borne by high autumn winds. And humankind fed the Gods with rich, flowing blood, and traced their images in starlight on the black dome of night.

***

You press your head against the door. The chant will not stop; the voices will not stop until the full tale is told. A young man's voice, passionate and angry, takes up the chant:

Then men looked to the deep places, and found metals there, and the metals served them. Gold they loved above all. They shaped it in honor of the Gods who made them, the Gods who taught them, the Gods who watched over them.

Chak Chel, face carven by cares, bearing always her great vessel, passed the fanged mouth of a river-laced cave into darkness. She came to Xibalba, the Underworld. She spoke to the Princes of the Under-Dark:

"Honored Gods of Under-Dark, man is wise. Humans know the Gods, they worship the Gods. Teach them your secrets. Lakes of quiescent liquid fire lie silent, deep in the Earth, where no spark may reach them. Grant humans this power that they might do great works upon the lands above. Let the oil, the black blood of the Earth, give men freedom and power worthy of their wisdom."

Among the hideous, whispering shapes gathered in the great Under-Dark, on his stone platform cushioned with many jaguar hides, their Lord leaned forward and regarded Chak Chel from beneath his feather-trimmed hat. His splendid brocade cape was of every color and splendid, and He blew smoke from a smoldering, hissing roll of dried tobacco. Toothless, He spoke:

"And what price will man pay? The black oil is precious, and more precious and potent still are other secrets beneath the Earth. I ask you, Chak Chel, what price will man pay?"

Then through smoke and shrouding gloom, Chak Chel met the Dark One's eyes and said:

"I swear to you Great One, if you give humans this power, they will use it wisely. They will honor you for this gift. As man has honored the land, the beasts and the sweet-tasting Maize, as he has honored the stars and the Sky, man will honor you: in his gratitude, he will quench your thirst with great goblets of warm blood."

And He of the deep places said:

"This and more shall man pay."

***

Footsteps above now, leaving the chamber, a few of them, moving toward the stairs. A small boy's voice takes over the chant now, hesitant and self-conscious:

So humans mastered the black oil of the Under-Dark. It drove them over the land, across the waters and atop the winds. With its power they shaped the

land to their liking. Their numbers grew and Chak
Chel watched as they spread like a rising tide over all
the Earth.

But the hearts of men turned, for they told
themselves they were masters over all. They lived like
locusts, consuming with a bottomless hunger. They
feared not beasts, nor Sky, nor Sea. In their pride, they
forgot to worship the Gods. They forgot to sacrifice to
the Gods. They forgot to fear the Gods.

Forgotten, the Gods grew weak. Long unfed by
the rich blood of sacrifice, they languished, each alone,
starved of their strength. As dark clouds gathered over
the Earth, the Gods gathered too in their high place.
The Gods of plants, of beasts, of Sky. All gathered, but
they were weak and their power was no longer over
man.

But one had not faltered; for man's births were
more than ever. She watched over each one and fed
upon the blood of these births, and blind hope, too,
kept her strong. From their high place the Gods called
her to them. They called Chak Chel. She had
journeyed long, great Mother of all men; her age was
upon her, and her face was gaunt.

Jaguar-God spoke:

"Chak Chel, man has thrived; it is as you
wished. He rules over the land, his numbers grow
without cease, and my children are now few. Soon
their cries will echo only in man's hollow tales of ages
gone."

Maize-God spoke:

"Chak Chel, man has great power. It is as you
wished. He rules over the green drinkers of sunlight,
and of my many children in their rapturous array of
shapes and colors, he has kept only a favored few alive,

twisting their hidden souls to glut his own appetites.
The rest will never again stretch their slender arms
toward the sun."

Itzamna, Lord of Sky, Father of All, spoke:

"Chak Chel, man has great knowledge. It is as
you wished. The secrets of the stars are his, but he has
violated his trust. He has broken the bounds of the
Sky, he has dared venture among moon and stars."

Then the Nameless One came, wrapped in
listless smoke, face unseen beneath his hat of many
feathers, and He said:

"All is as you wished. Humans have delved into
the depths, taken the iron, the gold, the black oil. They
have plundered all the treasures of the Under-Dark,
leaving a vast emptiness."

Jaguar-God spoke again and though his sleek
coat was now worn as a well-trodden pelt-rug, his
yellow eyes still glittered, even under the dark clouds.

"Mankind made promises to us: oaths of
reverence, oaths of blood. But man has forgotten his
oaths. And Chak Chel, honored Goddess whose waters
nourish all life, mankind has forgotten you."

***

*They are at the door. Now they silently enter the room, four
masked figures with torches, their thirsty eyes fixed on you.
You wish with all your strength that the Canticle would go
on longer -- hours, days, please, please, let them keep
chanting for a month, a whole year. But every story has its
end. The four masked ones murmur along as in the room
above, a small girl's voice rings out, melodious, excited:*

Chak Chel, so forceful in argument, heard all and
was silent. In her silence was sorrow, and her head
bowed. Her stout figure shook and all believed she
wept. But her trembling was the tremor of a coming

storm; and when She raised her head, her eyes were aboil. With her rage the heavens darkened and the Earth grew hot.

Then Chak Chel raised her great vessel and said:

"Man is born from water, every one from water, and in water he shall meet his end."

The waters of her vessel began to shudder, wild for release, and Chak Chel poured those great waters onto the Earth.

The tameless Sea rose, higher and higher, its force surpassing all measure or means. The waters rose over man's proud works, beating at their foundations and washing clean his folly. The heat of Chak Chel's anger scorched and withered the Earth's glorious coat of green, and from her rage sprang plagues and war to purge man's pride. But humankind had forgotten the names of the Gods; their howls were as the baying of wild dogs, their cries like the screeching of monkeys as the Sea swallowed our mothers and fathers and drank up even their screams.

A few remembered Chak Chel, though, the wisest few -- they remembered her name from the ancient tales. They set her carven image in a place of reverence, they remembered what she thirsted for. They fed her with sacrifice, with streams of rich red blood.

Then at last, Chak Chel's rage relented. Before all the sons and daughters of man were consumed, Chak Chel's vengeance cooled. She drew her great vessel to her breast and the waters grew still. A blessed silence blanketed the Earth.

And today, as in our earliest beginnings, our lives belong to Chak Chel's mercy, we few who

remain, we whose mothers and fathers the waters did
not swallow. We few, we praise Chak Chel, we fear
Chak Chel, and each time the moon blackens and dies
in the Sky, each night like this one, we feed Chak
Chel's hunger with the blood of those who did not
believe. And we sing that we might never again forget:

***

All sing:
Chak Chel, sacred Mother
Chak Chel, who gives life
Her mercy alone stays the all-drinking Sea
Chak Chel watches still as each new-born, each child
Each man and each woman draws breath on this Earth

And so it ends.

2012 AUTHORS

Lyn Cannaday lives in Arizona where she is a nationally recognized teacher by day. She enjoys torturing students with Washington Irving, Sophocles, Poe and all the macabre tales that emotionally damaged her as a young woman. She writes at night after grading hundreds of essays in red ink. Her stories have appeared in Alien SkinMagazine, Apollo's Lyre, Pen Pricks, Flashshots, and most recently in MorpheusTales and Crossed Genres Magazine.

Nancy Chenier currently lives and writes in Japan, under the delusion that she might escape impending doom by taking refuge in the more amiable pantheon of the Far East. It won't help her. Until then, you can find some of her stories in *Lilith Unbound* (, ed.), *The Book of Exodi* (Michael , ed) and in past issues of *OnSpec*.

Steven R. **Southard** scribbles tales in various genres: science fiction, steampunk, historical, horror, and fantasy. After serving in the submarine force and later working as a naval engineer, his creative right brain screamed for mercy and he began writing. Now he can't stop, and he loves every moment of this new endeavor. You're holding the fourth anthology in which one of his stories appears. Surf to http://sites.google.com/site/stevenrsouthard/where you can submerge into Steve's amazing world. Naturally, he has no plans for anything after December 2012.

"**Chad** is a biologist who moonlights as an author of short stories and poetry, including contributions to the publications House of Horror and The Garden of Life. He has also published scientific articles in journals such as Apoptosis, Biology of Reproduction, and Hepatology – medical research is his day job. He is an American Southerner but now lives in Oxford, England."

Wendy N. Wagner lives, works and prepares for the zombie apocalypse in Portland, Oregon. She is currently a contributing blogger and reviewer for Horor-Web.com, and also blogs at http://operabuffo.blogspot.com.

A writer for most of her life, **Jennifer Greylyn** has only recently been persuaded by the thoughtful but not very subtle prompting of family and friends that other people might enjoy her work as well. Her stories have appeared in, among other other places, the zines Abyss and Apex and Bards and Sages Quarterly and the anthologies Lilith Unbound, Malpractice: Tales of Bedside Terror and The Book of Exodi and more stories are forthcoming in the zines Beneath Ceaseless Skies and Neo-opsis as well as the vampire anthology, Evolve. She writes under a pseudonym to keep her writing life separate from her more mundane existence as a university teacher and tutor. She lives in Canada and expects 2012 to be a very interesting year.

Jenny Ashford is a writer and graphic artist from central Florida. Her work has appeared in several anthologies including ChimeraWorld #3, ChimeraWorld #4, and History Is Dead; her story "The Anatomy Lesson" earned an honorable mention in the 2008 edition of The Year's Best Fantasy and Horror. Her first book of short stories, Hopeful Monsters, was published in September 2009. She also writes articles on science, history and the arts for

Suite101.com. For more information, visit her website at www.jennyashford.com

Jason Colavito is an author, editor, and skeptical xenoarchaeologist who studies the intersection of horror fiction and (pseudo)science. He has written several books about the horror genre, including *The Cult of Alien Gods: H. P. Lovecraft and Extraterrestrial Pop Culture* (Prometheus, 2005) and *Knowing Fear: Science, Knowledge, and the Development of the Horror Genre* (McFarland, 2008), and covered the alternative archaeology movement both online and in the pages of *Skeptic* magazine. Colavito lives in New York State.

Trent Roman is a writer from Montréal with an interest in all types of fiction strange and unusual in addition to academic interests in archaeology, anthropology, history and a number of other fields. He is fascinated by what makes people tick at both the intimately personal level and the sweeping societal level, and enjoys every opportunity to pursue such questions through the means of fiction.

David A. Hewitt was born in Germany, raised outside Chicago, and spent eight years in Japan studying Japanese language and classical martial arts. As a freelance translator of Japanese, his credits include the animated feature *Blade of the Phantom Master* and the animated series *Welcome to the NHK*, *Area 88*, and *Gilgamesh*. A recent graduate of the University of Southern Maine's Stonecoast MFA program in Popular Fiction, he now lives in Maryland, USA, where he teaches English and Japanese at Carroll Community College and the Community College of Baltimore County. He is currently at work on his first novel.

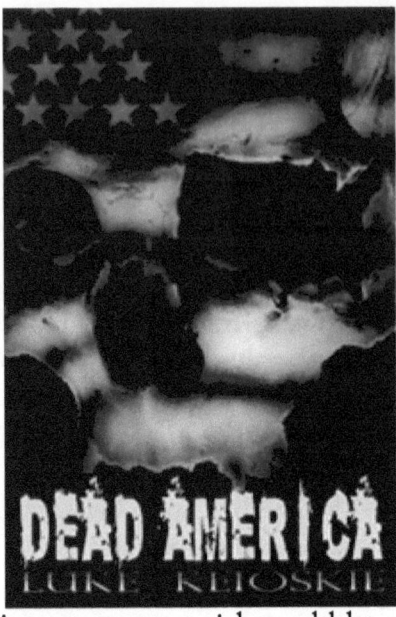